Frustration steamed from his obsidian eyes.

An ungentlemanly curse growled from the depths of his throat, and while I watched this jungle display in disbelieving fascination, his hand flashed out and gripped my wrist. He crushed me against the unyielding wall of his chest. My one yelp of outrage was silenced by his lips, which found mine with the swift, unerring accuracy of a hawk seizing its prey.

His angry growl softened to a reassuring croon, which was more devastating than those lips that flamed on mine and the pressure of his strong body. Something inside me melted at the exquisite intimacy of that sound, coming from inside him.

I gave up all hope of escape, or of wanting to, and abandoned myself to his primitive lovemaking. . . .

Also by Joan Smith
Published by Fawcett Books:

LADY MADELINE'S FOLLY
LOVE BADE ME WELCOME
MIDNIGHT MASQUERADE
THE MERRY MONTH OF MAY
COUSIN CECILIA
WINTER WEDDING
ROMANTIC REBEL
THE WALTZING WIDOW
THE NOTORIOUS LORD HAVERGAL
BATH SCANDAL
JENNIE KISSED ME
THE BAREFOOT BARONESS

Chapter One

It was just one week after my father's death when we sat that afternoon in the saloon at Gracefield discussing it. We couldn't let it go. It kept nagging like a sore tooth. And like a sore tooth, the problem was destined to get worse before we were through with it.

"What I keep wondering," I said, "is what he was doing in Brighton in the first place, when he said he was going to London. Papa had no earthly reason to be in Brighton, Bunny."

My companion and cousin, Mr. Horatio Smythe, shook his head in mute wonder. Mr. Smythe had been nicknamed Bunny at Harrow, and though he had, at twenty-five, outgrown the nervous twitch of the nose which had given birth to the name, he remained an amiable, gentle creature, whose worst fault was his lack of conversation. "Boggles the mind," he agreed.

He took a sip of ale and looked around for a subject to distract me. I needed cheering. Papa had not only gone to Brighton when he should have been at London; he had died there, under mysterious circumstances. He was never sick a day in his life, and was only fifty years old. Not a colt precisely, but still he had always been a hale and hearty gentleman.

Bunny glanced around the saloon of Gracefield, my family's estate on the coast of Kent. It loomed large in his mind that I was now the sole owner of the estate. To cheer me, he had already mentioned a few times that Gracefield was "a dandy place, with hundreds of acres and a good income." The saloon we sat in was quietly elegant, though a touch too blue to suit me. I like cheerful rooms.

"All yours now, Heather," he said once again. "A dashed heiress. Good thing we're first cousins, or Mama would make me dangle after you."

Bunny spent more time at Gracefield than at his own home three miles away. It was the arguing females that drove him out of Seaview. No man should be saddled with three sisters, unless they were all three mutes. All the neighbors let Bunny run quite tame in their saloons. He was no menace to their daughters' virtue or reputations.

"There is something so very *odd* about it," I continued, "almost as though someone was trying to deceive us. The funeral wagon that brought the coffin was from London, and the doctor's bill was from London. But the man who brought back his carriage and horses let slip they had been stabled in Brighton."

"Could have lent his rattler and prads to someone. A friend," Bunny suggested.

"That is what we thought, but then just this morning his traveling case arrived from the Royal

Crescent Hotel in Brighton. Aunt Lovatt burst into tears on the spot, so I had the servants take it away at once for Williams to unpack."

"Wits are gone begging, Heather. Ask Williams what your papa was doing at Brighton. His valet will know."

"Williams did not go with him. Papa always went alone to London. And that is odd, too, for you know he was always a little proud of his appearance."

"Regular peacock. Ah!" Bunny lifted his ale to hide the smirk that decorated his blushing face.

He only crops out into that particular shade of rose when he is thinking things he shouldn't about women. I wonder why the first thing that pops into a man's mind when some strange behavior arises is that a woman is involved.

"There is no lady in the case," I told him.

"Didn't say there was."

"Your smirk said it."

"By the living jingo, you have a mind like a steel sieve, Heather. Er—trap. You know what I mean. Thing is, why not take Williams, unless he was trying to keep something mum? Knew that clapper jaw of a Williams would tell Mrs. Gibbons. Mrs. Gibbons would tell your aunt. Even the best-intentioned servants blab everything they know."

"I wonder if there might be a clue in his traveling case," I said, frowning. The whole affair of my father's death was deeply troubling. Since Mama's death three years before, Papa had become a self-absorbed man. He was not close to either me or his sister, Mrs. Lovatt, who lived with us.

His hobby for some years had been breeding and training racing pigeons. After Mama's death, the hobby grew into a passion. He hired a live-in expert named Snoad to help him. A sly, encroaching man. I usually only saw Papa at mealtimes, and often not even then. It was by no means unusual for him to have a tray taken up to the pigeon loft.

That being the case, I had not thought I would miss him so much. Some lingering guilt added to my malaise. Papa and I had had a flaming row. It was ostensibly over his refusal to allow me a Season in London, but in truth, the real cause was his mistress. Mama died within a year of learning about Mrs. Mobley. I felt Mrs. Mobley contributed to her decline, and in the heat of battle, I threw it in Papa's face. Things were never the same between us after that.

If I had been a better companion for Papa, we would have been closer. His death seemed to cut everything off in the middle, and leave business unfinished between us. I had not even said good-bye the day he left. He liked an early departure. He had already left at eight when I came downstairs that morning a week ago.

"Ask Williams to bring the case down," Bunny suggested.

I sent off for Williams. The valet came, wearing an air of injury. "I have been packing your father's belongings, as Mrs. Lovatt requested, Miss Hume," he said.

"Have you unpacked his traveling case yet, Williams?

"I have not gotten around to it, ma'am. I am at present stuffing his boots with paper and giving them a final touch of polish."

"What are you doing with them?" Bunny asked.

"They are to go to the parish home, sir."

"Good," Bunny said approvingly. He was on the Parish Council, and took a keen interest in his job.

"Send down Papa's case. I'll look through it myself," I said.

Williams sniffed and replied, "Very well, Miss Hume, if you cannot wait an hour or two."

"You won't be sorry to see the back of that toplofty customer," Bunny said. "Mean to say, no point keeping a valet when his master is—er—gone." I had noticed that people had difficulty saying the word "dead."

"Mrs. Lovatt has given him a month to look about for another position. He was with Papa for five years. We cannot just toss him out on his ear, much as we may like to."

It was the parlor maid who entered moments later, carrying a leather traveling case with brass corners and lock pad. Bunny placed it on the sofa table and opened it. "Not locked," he mentioned. "I always lock mine when I'm traveling."

"The hotel would not have had the key. It was in a small box containing Papa's watch and wallet and jewelry that came with his body from London. But this case from Brighton proves that Papa *was* there. This is his case."

Bunny lifted out a blue jacket of Bath cloth. "This is his coat, right enough," he said.

"And that is his shirt," I added, lifting out a white shirt whose buttons had been moved by my own hand when Papa put on a few pounds. I shook it out. "What on earth is this dirt on it!" I exclaimed. A brown smear on the left side stood out in sharp relief against the white. I stared in dismay as I realized what it was. Blood! "Good God! He must have been wounded. Look at this, Bunny."

Bunny's face had turned yellow. It wasn't the shirt he was looking at, but the jacket. I looked to see what had caught his attention. There was a small hole in the back, on the left side. His stubby fingers moved over the hole, which had certainly been made by a bullet. I turned the shirt over to examine the back. It, too, was bloodstained, though not so much as the front. Then I saw the little round hole. We exchanged a frightened look. "He was shot!" I said, on a light squeak of disbelief.

"I feared there was a woman in the case," Bunny said. "No point trying to keep it from you now. Fat's in the fire. Must have been a duel. Perhaps she was married."

"What woman? What are you talking about?"

"Your papa trotting off without his valet. Regular as clockwork every two weeks. He must have had a ladybird."

"I don't believe it," I scoffed. "He never looked at another woman after Mama's death." Bunny just looked at me. The name Mrs. Mobley hung in the air between us.

"I heard she went to Ireland," Bunny said. "Must be a new charmer."

"He did not go to London every two weeks to visit a lady. He went on pigeon business."

"Yes, but think, Heather. How long had he been taking these trips?"

"About two years. They began a year after Mama's death," I added pensively. It struck me as a likely period for celibate mourning of a wife. "But why did he say he was going to London?"

"Had to have some excuse."

"The story he told us was that he was going to meetings of the Columbidae Society, but he could have let on the meetings were in Brighton just as well. I wonder if he has a picture of her." I began rooting through the case. Sox, cravats, and small cloths were churned up and fell to the floor. A smaller leather case held his razor and brushes. I pulled them out with trembling fingers. There was no picture. There was nothing in the whole traveling case to give any clue to the mysterious woman Bunny spoke of.

"There's nothing," I said, and felt disappointed, when I ought to have been relieved. "But he really did go to those pigeon society meetings, Bunny. He sold his racers, and bought birds from the other breeders. He always took a dozen pigeons with him, and brought other birds home. He would not go to all that bother just to meet his mistress."

"Killing two birds with one stone," Bunny suggested.

"I'll speak to Snoad."

But not yet. I was too shaken to stand up, let alone climb three flights of stairs to the loft. I had to examine the shirt and jacket again, to finger the little holes and try to imagine my father being so dashing as to have a mistress, and being involved in a duel. It was true Papa was a dasher in his youth. Mama often spoke of it, boasted of it really, but I had never seen any signs of it except the brief affair with Mrs. Mobley. The last few years, my papa had seemed as tame as Bunny. In fine weather he went shooting on his own or neighboring estates, but most of his time he spent on his pigeons.

Training the birds was a very cumbersome affair. The birds had to be taken to points distant from the loft, to train them to return. They began with a short distance, a mile or less, gradually increasing it to greater lengths. Snoad and my father shared the duty, one taking the birds, the other remaining in the loft to time the return.

"Papa was a good shot. It's odd he did not win that duel," I said. I looked again at the holes and the stains. A frisson scuttled across my scalp. "Look, Bunny."

"A terrible thing, dueling," he said grimly.

"Yes, and *murder* is worse. The bullet holes are in the back of the jacket and shirt. They did not come out the front. The bullet was lodged in his body. It was not a duel. Papa was murdered."

Bunny's mouth fell open. "By gad, you're right. Shot in the back, like a dog. I was so shocked at seeing the blood, I didn't notice where the holes were at first."

Nor had I. "What should I do? I must notify the constable."

"We'll drive in to Hythe," he said. Gracefield was two miles outside of the bustling seaport city of Hythe.

I remembered having my purse stolen from the counter in the drapery shop at Hythe a year before. I had described the thief in detail to the constable, but she had never been apprehended. Just how would a constable from Hythe find a murderer in Brighton? "No, to Brighton," I said.

"Eh?"

"Brighton. That is where he was killed."

"That's more than fifty miles away."

"I don't care if it's fifty hundred. I must go." At last there was something I could do for Papa.

"You're right, of course. A bit late to leave today. We'll go tomorrow."

I looked a question at him. "You'll come with me?"

"Can't go alone," he said simply.

Nor could I go alone with a gentleman. "Aunt Lovatt will accompany me, but we will be very happy for your escort, Bunny. You will be better able to deal with constables and so on than Auntie and I."

"Least I can do. First cousins, after all. Your mama and mine were sisters. Don't see how Mama can talk me out of it, and it will be good to get away from those squabbling girls for a few days."

"I must break the news to Aunt Lovatt," I said reluctantly.

At that moment a brisk, no-nonsense lady of middle years strode into the saloon. She was a thin, wiry female with more of health than beauty. The edge of hair showing beneath her widow's cap was brown, just shading to silver. Her sharp green eyes wore the luster of intelligence. She had come to live with Papa when Mama died. I, at sixteen, had been considered too green to run the house. At first I set my jaw against her, but in the end we rubbed along very well.

She was not so very different from me, barring the difference in years. I tended to favor my father's side of the family. In twenty years I expect my brown hair will have silvered like hers. The fine claws of Mr. Crow will have marked the corners of my green eyes, too. Unless I run to fat like my mother's side of the family, I expect I shall have a similar figure.

As Mrs. Lovatt was a childless widow, she had welcomed the offer to live with us. I soon filled the hole in her life left by her lack of children. She could not have loved me more had I been her own flesh and blood. Neither of us was the maudlin sort who prated of love, but genuine affection was there in plentiful supply.

"Good day, Mr. Smythe," she smiled. "What must you break to Aunt Lovatt, Heather?" she asked, turning a sharp eye in my direction. She saw the open case, and drew back a step. "Those are Harold's things?" she asked.

"Yes, I asked Williams to send them down," I replied. "Sit down, Auntie. I'm afraid you will receive a dreadful shock."

Aunt Lovatt's face turned quite pale. She sank onto a chair, clutching her heart. Papa's death had been shock enough for one spring. The mystery of his carriage coming from Brighton had added to it, and just when we had decided that he had lent the rig to someone, his traveling case had come landing in from Brighton. Now I had to tell her about the murder.

Aunt Lovatt saw the brown stain on the white shirt, and knew at once that Papa had not died a natural death, as the report had stated. Heart failure, the death certificate had said. And the body already nailed into a sealed coffin to hide the truth. My aunt had insisted on having the coffin opened. It had seemed so incredible that Papa was dead. We had stood with the undertaker, just long enough for one peek at Papa's rigid, livid face. Then we had both turned away without even glancing at the rest of him.

"Was he stabbed?" she asked through grim lips.

"Shot," Bunny said, and rose for the wine decanter. He poured Mrs. Lovatt a glass and handed it to her. He waited until she had taken a sustaining sip before adding, "In the back."

"Murdered!" Mrs. Lovatt gasped.

"Yes, Auntie, and that is why we must go to Brighton to look into this," I said.

"Of course," she said at once. "We cannot leave it hanging like this. We must discover who did this heinous thing, and see he is punished." We three exchanged silent looks of dread. "We shall leave early tomorrow morning," she said.

"Bunny has offered to accompany us," I told her.

"How very kind of you, Mr. Smythe." Tears glazed her eyes. She rose on unsteady legs and said, "I shall ask the maid to remove the valise. Perhaps you will put your father's things back into it, Heather. We'll take it to Brighton with us for evidence."

"I'll handle it," I said, patting her arm.

"Poor Heather," she said, with tears in her eyes. I knew what was in her mind as she turned and went up to her room. She would be brooding over how this affair would affect my matrimonial chances. Like a concerned mother, she had hoped to see me make a grand match. I was becoming a trifle old to make my bows in London, but there were less demanding cities. Bath, for instance, received many visitors from the ton, and she had a wide field of connections there, where she had lived for many years. She had mentioned the visit before Papa's death, and while she was too refined to speak of it so soon after, I knew she meant to go after our year of mourning.

But a girl whose father had caused a scandal wouldn't stand a chance of being accepted in staid Bath. Perhaps we could keep the inquiry quiet. A few discreet questions at the hotel first, to see just what Papa had been up to, that he got himself killed. Very likely a woman *was* involved. Papa was still young enough to want female companionship. Or it might have been a card game with a Captain Sharp. That, while disastrous, at least cast no slur on Papa or his daughter. Any gentleman might fall amongst thieves.

But why the chicanery about moving his body to London before sending it home? There was something deep going on here. We must proceed with the greatest caution.

Chapter Two

When Aunt Lovatt left, Bunny said, "You was going to have a word with Snoad. Might be a good idea to see if he knows anything."

"He'll be up in the loft."

"There's another servant you can be rid of," Bunny said, hoping to cheer me by thoughts of the saving in money. "What will you do with the pigeons?"

"I have no idea. If Mr. Pelletier were still here, he'd take them. It was Pelletier who got Papa interested. He was Belgian, you know. He returned home years ago. They are very keen on racing pigeons in Belgium. Perhaps Snoad will take them off my hands."

"Take them? Buy them, more like. Your papa paid a tidy sum for some of those birds, and sold the ones he bred. Don't let Snoad get the better of you, my girl."

"What on earth would I do with them?" I asked as we went toward the staircase.

It was a long climb. Papa had glazed the widow's walk of Gracefield, and turned it into a loft. It ran along the south facade of the mansion, looking across the Channel to France. From its lofty height the wives of the house of Hume had strained their eyes for a sight of their husbands' ships since the days of Queen Elizabeth. In spring the glazed panels had been raised, leaving only a wire mesh to keep the birds in. The door to the widow's walk opened onto a bartizan. The bartizan was unscreened and unglazed. From it, one could see for miles.

On a clear day the blue haze in the far distance was called France. On that afternoon, as on so many days on the coast of England, the air was foggy. The sea breeze carried a cold Atlantic moisture that penetrated my gown and laid waste my coiffure.

The cooing of pigeons was audible as soon as we entered the loft. Some birds had left their perches and strutted along the floor at their ungainly pigeon gait, necks extending at every step. Snoad kept the loft tidy, but a pigeon's feathers are easily dislodged, and one floated on the breeze. A dozen birds sat on various perches arranged for their comfort. The loft even boasted one tree, a miniature apple tree planted in a huge wooden barrel, which was the private preserve of a bird called Caesar, and which was occasionally shared by his mate, Cleo. The tree, I noticed, was empty that day.

The birds came in a wide variety of colors. Some were gray or brown, others glinted with iridescent hues of green and pink and gold. My father knew the pedigree of every one of the hundred plus pigeons, but truth to tell, I found it all a bore. I would have preferred if Papa had raised horses, or even parrots, if he must raise birds. Pigeons are such stupid-seeming birds. I knew that they were monogamous. I remembered that because it had seemed strange that these little balls of feathers mated for life, like people.

I also knew that the undisputed stars of the collection were Caesar and Cleo. Caesar raced, and Cleo was a breeder. Papa didn't usually race his breeders, although Cleo had won a few races in her youth.

A swarthy young man in shirt sleeves was examining some bags of feed at the far end of the loft. He turned to greet us with a curt "Good day." I never felt entirely comfortable with Snoad. There was something unsettling about the man. He did not dress as a servant should, for one thing, but wore a dilapidated jacket of blue worsted, which looked like the castoff of a gentleman. In warmer weather he wore shirt sleeves and sometimes a vest. He carried his wide shoulders in a swaggering motion. His flashing black eyes were too clever by half. He had never shown a proper respect to Papa, nor to me. Snoad was more than half the reason I came so seldom to the loft. Papa said he was the most knowledgeable man in England where pigeons were concerned, and no doubt that was why he gave himself airs.

It was typical of Snoad that he did not join us, but continued with his work, waiting for us to go to him. Nettled, I said, "I would like a word with you, Snoad."

"In a minute, miss," he said over his shoulder, and continued his work.

"I am in a hurry," I called sharply. It annoyed me that he called me miss instead of ma'am. I particularly disliked that he belittled me by his inattention in front of Bunny. Really, the man was insufferable. One would think he owned the loft.

Snoad turned and came forward at a leisurely gait, shoulders rolling as he walked. "What can I do for you, Miss Hume?" he asked. His accent was good, though where he had acquired it was a deep mystery. I knew that before coming to Gracefield, he had been employed by the Duke of Prescott, in Wiltshire, to tend his wife's aviary. If I had been the duke, I would not have let this man within a mile of the duchess.

"I have a few questions about Papa's last trip. Who was he seeing?" I asked.

"He was attending a meeting of the Columbidae Society," he replied, with a look that said, "as you very well know."

"No, he was not. Did he mention anyone in particular?"

"A Mr. Jones," Snoad said. He did not quite smirk, but there was an insolent unsteadiness about his lips.

"In Brighton, or London?"

"In London, miss."

"Would you have Mr. Jones's address?"

"No, miss. I'm afraid not."

"His first name?"

"Mr. George Jones, I believe."

After several decades of King Georges, George was the most common man's name in England, and Jones was not far behind. "It turns out that Papa was not in London at all," I said. "He was in Brighton. Whom did he sell to in Brighton?"

"In Brighton, you say?" he asked, mildly curious. "How did you hear that?"

I stared him out of countenance. "You can take my word for it. He was in Brighton. Whom did he sell to there?"

"No one, as far as I know."

"You must know something!" I said angrily. "You are supposed to be the expert."

"I *am* the expert, but I only train the darlings, Miss Hume. I don't sell them," he replied boldly.

"That is a pity," I said, raking him with my eyes. "I had hoped you might tell me whom I could profitably sell the collection to."

That jolted Snoad out of his insolence. "Sell them!" he exclaimed, eyes flashing. "You can't sell them!"

"Can I not? Papa left me his entire estate, which includes this loft. I shall sell the birds and pull this horrid wire down. It destroys the looks of the house."

"You can't!" he repeated, his voice louder than before.

"If you can come up with a name of a buyer, he might hire you, Snoad," I said, enjoying my victory. "You will not be needed here, once the birds are gone."

"But the birds would be useless anywhere else. Racers are trained to return to their own loft. This collection is extremely valuable, Miss Hume. Your father spent years building it up." He spoke earnestly, all haughtiness vanished.

"I am well aware that my father spent all his time and most of his money on this loft. I have other priorities. I shall be rid of the birds and dismantle the loft immediately," I said grandly.

Snoad rubbed his hand over his mouth in consternation. His dark eyes glowed with banked fires of frustration. "Don't do it yet," he said. "Give me a few weeks to make some arrangement. Somewhere else to take the birds."

"Did you wish to buy them then?" I asked. I would gladly give them to him to be rid of them, but only wanted to repay him for his impertinent behavior.

"Yes, I'll buy them," he replied, without a moment's hesitation.

"Said they was no good without this loft," Bunny reminded him.

"We have several valuable birds brooding. The new chicks could be trained from a different loft," he explained. "You must give me some time to make arrangements, Miss Hume."

"Are you quite sure you can afford to buy the collection, Snoad, as you speak of it as being so valuable?" I said. I had always been curious about this enigmatic man. Now it sounded as though he had more money than I would have thought. It immediately darted into my head that Papa was paying him too much.

It had been the cause of angry muttering between Aunt Lovatt and myself that Snoad had been given the entire top floor of the house. This consisted of only two rooms, to be sure, but they were large, bright rooms. Papa said he required a study for his scientific work. It was news to me that a man who cleaned out pigeon nests was a scientist.

The sly look had returned. "I pick up a few pounds on the races," Snoad replied. "Why, I might even make you an offer on Gracefield. I know you've always wanted a Season in London."

"So I have." I smiled, taking it for an attempt at humor. "But it will not be necessary for me to sell

Gracefield to have a Season. I shall be going to Brighton tomorrow, for a few days. You cannot give me any names of customers that I might speak to?"

His handsome face took on a conning expression. "Now, why would you want to do that, Miss Hume? I thought we'd agreed I'd buy the collection."

Bunny said, "Mr. Hume was murdered." I gave him a rebukeful look. "Don't see any point in keeping it mum. We're looking into it. Any help you can give us would be appreciated, Snoad."

Watching Snoad, I felt in my bones that he was not surprised at the announcement of my father's murder. He was wary, but he was not surprised. "Is that so?" he asked, brows rising over his sharp eyes. "Where did you get that notion, Mr. Smythe, if you don't mind my asking?"

"From the bullet hole in the back of his jacket."

Snoad considered this a moment in silence. "Where did the jacket come from?" he asked.

"The Royal Crescent Hotel, in Brighton."

"We mean to learn where the bullet hole came from, too," I told him.

Snoad gazed steadily into my eyes. There was some hypnotic force in his gaze. His eyes were so dark that even the whites of them looked an iridescent gray. "I'd be very careful if I were you, Miss Hume. It might be best not to go digging into it. I had a great respect for your father, but it's unusual for a man who is going about his own business to get himself murdered."

"Are you saying my father was involved in something dishonest!" I demanded.

"Not minding his own business was what I said. I'm not accusing him of anything dishonest. I believe your father's trips involved more than bird business, if you read my meaning." Something in his manner, or voice, suggested sexual doings. The eyes glinted recklessly, and his voice held an undertone of innuendo. Snoad always looked as if he had sex on his mind. It was one of the things about him that made me uneasy. One was always aware of being a woman when in his presence.

"You mean a woman?" Bunny asked bluntly. "Thought so m'self."

"Mr. Hume never said so, but I know he always packed his black suit and his dancing slippers when he went to London."

"But he was killed in Brighton," I said.

"So you say. If I had killed my wife's lover, I'd be at pains to muddy the waters a little. Moving the body is one way of doing it."

How naturally he said that. *If I had killed my wife's lover.* Murder was nothing to this man. Nor was taking another man's wife. I noticed his eyes were on me, and there was a spark of amusement, no doubt due to my shocked expression.

"I expect you would also have had the wits to take the carriage to London, with the victim's suitcase inside it," I sneered.

"So I would. Someone made a bad gaffe there. And you're off to Brighton, you say?"

"Yes, tomorrow morning."

"You'll require an escort." I took the absurd idea that Snoad was about to offer his services.

"I'm accompanying the ladies," Bunny said.

A vague smile tugged at Snoad's lips. "Excellent, Mr. Smythe. They will have no need of further assistance if you are along."

The tone of Snoad's voice was as good as a direct insult, but unsuspecting Smythe smiled in satisfaction. "Someone to deal with the constables," he mentioned.

"You'll be careful, Miss Hume," Snoad said. "Remember what I said." There was no smile now, nor any slyness.

I took a deep breath and said, "Do you know the lady's name, Snoad?"

"I could not even vouch that she was a lady, ma'am. Now, if you'll excuse me, the pigeons are waiting for their feed." He performed an easy, graceful bow, and returned to the sacks in the far corner, without waiting to be dismissed. I did not wish to risk further impertinence in front of Bunny, and let him go. I found myself wondering if he was a by-blow of the Duke of Prescott. There was an aristocratic arrogance in his manner. How could the Prescotts have endured his insolence unless he had some hold over them?

As he walked away, there was a rustle in the nests. A pink-necked bird flew from the perch and settled on his shoulder. "There now, Tess," he crooned, lifting a hand to gently stroke her wing. It was oddly uncharacteristic behavior from surly Snoad.

"That wasn't much help," I grouched, and returned belowstairs with Bunny. "I don't trust Snoad. Not as far as I could throw him."

"An oiler," Bunny added. "A foreign look about him. That dark hair and black eyes. Might be a gypsy."

"Yes, he has that sly air. If he had not been here the whole time Papa was gone, I could believe he had something to do with the murder. He must know something about Papa's customers. The two of them were close as inkle weavers."

"He mentioned that George Jones."

"There is no George Jones, Bunny."

"No George Jones?" Bunny gave a jeering look. "I daresay there are a hundred of them in London alone. Maybe more. Oh, heh heh. I see your meaning. Chose that name on purpose. Sly boots."

"Precisely. I wonder if Papa has any record of his customers in his study. Let us have a look."

Bunny glanced at his watch. "Time for me to be shabbing off home. Vicar's coming to dinner, thank God. The girls won't fight in front of him. They'll wait till he's gone, then they'll be at each other's throats. Beth and Mary are both sweet on him."

"You'll come early tomorrow morning?"

"I'll be here at eight-thirty. We'll take your rig. Your papa's prads are top o' the trees."

It was close to dinnertime, so I postponed my search of the office till later. After dinner, Mrs. Lovatt went upstairs to prepare for the visit to Brighton, and I went to my father's office, which was gradually becoming my office. I had had a deal of paperwork to do here, settling the details of my father's will. Soon I would be taking my father's place at those sessions with his bailiff, having to learn about tilling fields and rotating crops, and settling the tenants' account. I did not look forward to it with any eagerness, or any hope of pleasure. I began to understand why well-dowered ladies rushed into marriage.

Papa kept the estate books in a small desk in the corner. His pigeon records occupied pride of place at the large oak table desk in the center of the room. A ledger was there, open on the desk. I glanced at the columns, but they were not helpful. They merely listed the matings of birds, and probable time of hatching. Most of the words I didn't even understand. I had wondered what the Columbidae Society meant, and Papa had told me columbidae meant dove, which was the family that pigeons belonged to. I found myself liking our mourning doves less when I learned they were pigeons.

Papa had mated something called a Treroninaea with something else called a Ducula Aenea. The dates of breeding were listed with hatching to come, apparently two weeks to nineteen days later. Some of the hatch dates were listed. Usually two eggs, but sometimes only one survived. Another book had lists of feeds—seeds and cereal grains along with some green foods, and grit. He kept track of various diets he was trying on different birds, and the weight gain and flight times.

There was more than a lay person wanted to know about pigeons, but nothing to tell whom he sold them to. Surely there must be a ledger somewhere. I rooted through the drawers of his desk, but there was nothing. At the back of the bottom drawer I saw his pistol, always kept there. If he had taken it with him, perhaps he would be alive today. He had obviously not been expecting any trouble, or he would have taken it with him.

After half an hour's search, I was certain that the study had nothing to tell me. I was just about to extinguish the lamps when the door, which was ajar, opened, and Snoad entered. He gave a start of surprise.

"What are you doing here?" he demanded, in the accents of authority.

"I was about to ask you the same thing, Snoad. A gentleman usually knocks before entering a lady's room." That was a foolish thing to say. Snoad was no gentleman.

"I'll remember that advice, miss," he said, and came in. "You weren't sporting your oak."

"I beg your pardon?"

"The door was not actually closed." He closed it softly behind him, and advanced toward me.

For no sensible reason, I felt a sudden rush of panic.

Chapter Three

"You may leave the door ajar, Snoad," I said, with as much self-control as I could muster.

"Very well, if you're afraid, miss," he replied with a taunting smile, and opened it a crack.

"It is no odds. I find it a little close in here." His bold eyes skimmed off the shawl hugging my shoulders. "What is it you wanted?"

He advanced directly to the desk. A lazy smile moved across his lips, and when he spoke, his voice was smooth and rich, like Devonshire cream. "Why, I want to help you, miss. I thought I might find your father's list of customers, as you're so eager to have it."

"It's not here. I've looked all over."

"I've a few other things I wanted to check out as well. With you father gone, the running of the loft is in my care. I must see what feed he's ordered. The present supply won't last longer than a week. You wouldn't want those valuable birds to perish."

It was a rational answer, yet I felt in my bones

that it was not the truth. Snoad had come here to snoop. I would let him have any legitimate records he required, and then I would lock the door. Or better, have the lock changed, in case he had got hold of a key. Snoad might have the run of the loft, but he would not have the run of this office.

I handed him a heavy ledger. "I believe this is what you're looking for." He took the book, apparently recognizing it as the right one. No doubt he was familiar with it. "I don't know what Father's arrangements for paying were, but you may order what you require, and give me the bill."

"Thank you, Miss Hume," he said. His tone was humble, but those flashing eyes made a jest of humility.

"Was there anything else?" I asked, shuffling papers as if I were busy.

Snoad just stood, gazing around the room. He shook his head sadly. "I just wanted to come here and think about your father. We spent so many hours here, discussing plans. I miss him."

His tone was wistful, and for once, it was not at odds with his demeanor. It occurred to me that perhaps Snoad was genuinely saddened, even lonesome. He seldom saw anyone but my father and the visitors who came on bird business. Any breeder visiting in the vicinity of Gracefield was bound to call. Some gentlemen came from London for no other reason than to visit the loft and meet my father. Papa had written widely on his hobby, and gained some small degree of fame.

It was a strangely isolated life for a young man like Snoad. He was not treated as part of the family by any means. I knew he had some friends amongst the footmen and maids, but he was not precisely like them either. He was in the same awkward class as a governess: too high to be at home with the servants, and too low to mix freely with the family. Being a man, he had more freedom to go about the neighborhood, but other than the bird-training trips, I did not think he made much use of that freedom.

"Many a happy hour we have spent, over a bottle of wine," Snoad said. "Your father showed me his trophies for races won." He glanced to the bookcase along the far wall, where a small array of undistinguished cups and one silver-plated trophy in the shape of a pigeon rested.

"I miss him, too," I said. I took the decision to give Snoad some memento of my father, a watch or some such thing. For the past two years, Snoad had been closer to him than anyone else, including Aunt Lovatt and myself. "I would like you to have a keepsake of Papa, Snoad."

His eyes moved from the trophies to me. He seemed very much surprised at this friendly gesture. "You are very kind. I would treasure whatever you think fit to give me."

"Is there any particular item that has meaning for you? Perhaps his watch . . ."

Snoad considered it a moment. "I should, perhaps, mention, Miss Hume, Williams has already given me your father's boots."

"His boots!" I exclaimed.

"Not as a memento," he said. A slight blush rose up from his collar. "We happen to wear the same size. Your father had just had a new pair of Hessians made. It seemed . . ."

I was embarrassed for him. Snoad was a proud man, and was ashamed to be caught begging a pair of boots. "I meant a more lasting momento, Snoad," I said gently.

"Perhaps the gold watch fob in the shape of a pigeon," he suggested.

"I know the one you mean. I'll see that you get it." I was insensibly flattered at his choice, as I had had the trinket made for my father's birthday.

His obvious pleasure was ample reward for my generosity. Snoad was not the man to shed a tear, but I felt he was not far from it at this moment. "You are very kind," he said. Then he bowed and left abruptly.

I sat on alone, thinking. Perhaps I had misjudged Snoad. If he seemed uppity, it was no doubt due to inexperience with ladies. He was the blatantly handsome sort of man with a crude, superficial charm that would appeal to a certain class of woman. No doubt he had plentiful experience with women, but that was something else. As I was feeling kindly toward him, I did not bother to lock the office when I left, nor did I arrange to have the lock changed.

"Not sporting your oak," he had said. A strange expression, but one I had heard somewhere before. Ah, Pelletier! That was who said it. "A term I picked up at Oxford," he had mentioned when I asked about it. No doubt Snoad had heard it from the duke's family at Branksome Hall, and wished to ornament his conversation with this verbal trinket.

I sent a maid off to Williams for my father's watch fob. When the maid brought it, it was attached to the watch. I had no earthly use for Papa's watch. It was too large for a lady. I would give both watch and fob to Snoad, as a present. I meant to present it formally. The next thought was that Aunt Lovatt would raise the roof beams at the very idea of giving Snoad such a valuable gift.

Her disapproval lent the undertaking an aura of intrigue. Mrs. Lovatt seldom spoke to Snoad; she was not likely to hear of the gift. As we were leaving for Brighton the next morning, I decided to make the presentation that same evening. I could not go to Snoad's room, and disliked to have him sent for. I don't know why I balked at that. He was a servant, but he was not a regular house servant. He had worked exclusively for Papa. It occurred to me that he might be at the loft, and I took the gift up the two flights of stairs to check.

My patent slippers made little sound. The loft door was ajar, and I pushed it open wider. A faint aroma of cigar smoke wafted toward me, barely discernible over the pungent sea scent, but enough to tell me Snoad was there. I didn't know he smoked. Really I knew remarkably little about him, when one considered that we had lived under the same roof for two years. My father liked cheroots; perhaps Snoad had caught the habit from him.

In the silver light from the moon, I saw a man's outline, limned in black against the mesh grating. It made a romantic sort of silhouette. A proud, well-shaped head was staring out at the night. Snoad was at the trap by which the pigeons left and returned to the loft. He murmured something in a crooning voice, and I realized that he held a bird cupped in his fingers. He opened the trap and let it out. There was a soft flutter of wings, and the pigeon streaked off, first toward the sea, then it got its bearings and headed north. Snoad looked around warily, as if sensing an intruder.

"Snoad," I called, before he caught me spying on him.

He turned with a convulsive jerk. "Miss Hume?" he called.

"Yes, I hope I didn't frighten you."

"Not at all. Has something happened?" he asked, hurrying along the parapet toward me.

"No. I'm sorry if I alarmed you. Is this not an odd time of day—or night—to be releasing a pigeon?"

"They must learn to fly and keep their bearings at all hours, and in all weather." He looked at his cheroot, and extinguished it under his foot before I could stop him.

"You didn't have to do that. I don't mind cheroots. Papa used to smoke them."

"Yes, he gave me a box of his."

I cleared my throat for the presentation. "You were very close to my father, Snoad. He spoke highly of you. I'm sure he would want you to have something to remember him by. I want you to take this." I handed him the watch.

Our fingers met and fumbled together in the darkness. It was a strangely touching moment, not entirely devoid of romance. I pictured myself a Lady Bountiful, bequeathing a treasure on a serf.

Snoad took the watch and examined it, smiling. "I only meant the pigeon fob," he said, drawing something out of his pocket. "I have never seen another like it."

"It is unique. I had it made for my father."

"I know."

I pondered this reply, wondering if it had any significance. "But what good is a fob without a watch?" I said blandly. I saw then that what he held was a watch. Fancy Snoad having a watch!

"Oh, you already have one!" I said, a little vexed that my munificence was unnecessary. But his would not be so fine as Papa's, which was gold-plated.

"The duchess gave me this when I left Branksome Hall." He slid it in his pocket and attached my father's watch in its place. "It is a fine gold watch, but it has not the sentimental value of your father's timepiece for me, Miss Hume. I shall always treasure this." His voice was rough with emotion.

My nose was out of joint that his own watch was gold, but I was somewhat mollified by his words and tone. "I'm glad you like it," I said.

The meeting was over, yet I was loath to leave. There was some charm in the loft, with the big white moon silvering the ocean, and painting the landscape in ghostly hues. The cooing of pigeons and gentle flutter from the nests was an undercurrent to the sighing of the wind, and the breaking of waves on the shore below. "It's pretty up here," I said.

His smile, when he spoke, was not far removed from flirtation. "I have often regretted that you so seldom come to visit the birds."

"Papa never encouraged me to. He said I disturbed them."

"Ladies oftimes have a disturbing effect," he said. His tone said that their effect was not limited to birds.

I ignored his reply entirely. I had come upstairs without my shawl, and the sea breeze was chilly. I began rubbing my arms to keep warm.

"You're cold. Let me get you something to put on."

"I should go downstairs."

"What is the rush, Miss Hume? Now that you are here, why not enjoy the view for a moment?" He looked around, but finding no shawl or blanket to offer, he removed his own jacket and hung it over my shoulders.

His body heat was still in it, warming my back and arms. "Are you sure you don't need it yourself?" I asked.

"Quite sure. This gives me an opportunity to display my virility," he said facetiously.

We exchanged a smile, but I was quite aware of the virility in his broad, straight shoulders. His shirt showed them off to advantage. I noticed his stomach was board-flat, and his hips were trim. Moonlight played over the rugged planes of his face, casting his eyes into shadows, and highlighting his well-sculpted nose and sensuous lips. I began to wonder what else the duchess had given him, besides a gold watch. This was the sort of man who caused scandals in polite households.

"You look beautiful in the moonlight, Miss Hume," he said softly.

I warmed to his praise, but realized the situation was not at all proper, and depressed him with a joke. "I am one of those ladies who shows to best advantage in a dim light."

"I cannot agree with that. It's a pity it's nighttime, or I'd give you a tour of the place," he said. "We have a few nestlings. You might enjoy to see the chicks being fed. A strange way they have of nursing. Pigeons' milk comes from the crop of not only the mother, but the father as well. The hatchlings are fed milk for a week."

"The father nurses, too! How strange!" I said, happy to see he was not bent on flirtation.

"It is unique in nature, so far as I know. The fathers also share the incubation. They take the day shift, the mothers the night. That always seems ungentlemanly to me. The ladies ought to be allowed their beauty sleep. But it is foolish to judge them by human standards."

"What gives the birds such a variety of colors? Papa called the prettily colored ones fruit pigeons, I think."

"Yes, ordinary street pigeons are drab, like the rock pigeons that are the basis of all racing birds. With so much mixing of breeds, you often see a pretty pink or green glaze on street pigeons as well. The fruit pigeons come from all over—Asia, Africa, the South Pacific islands. They are such strong flyers, they've spread all over the world, in a bewildering assortment of crossbreeds."

"Caesar, I think, is our best flyer?"

"Perhaps the best in England. Your father's Belgian friend, Pelletier, provided the chick before he left the country. Pelletier claims to have birds that can fly two thousand miles."

"Goodness! I thought the races were only a hundred miles long."

"No, sometimes as far as five hundred miles. Those races are difficult to arrange in times of war. It involves taking the birds five hundred miles away, and timing their return. We only race from Edinburgh—about three hundred miles. After the war is over, I expect we'll see a great interest in pigeon racing."

"I doubt it will ever replace horse racing."

"It appeals to a different sort of person, a more

imaginative sort, I like to think. It is almost magical, in a way, to think a bird can soar through the sky for two thousand miles and always find its way home. That is quite a feat of navigation. Dobbin is not capable of that."

I was transported in my mind to that endless silver sky, arcing over vast continents. "It must be a wonderful sensation to fly through the air, looking down on life below. If I were a bird, I'd fly to Persia or Peru, and never return."

"You are more romantical than I had thought," he said, with a close look.

"I wonder what makes the birds come back."

"We don't really know. The loft is their home, where they were born and bred. They know food and safety are here, and in some cases, but not always, the mate. We have bachelors and maiden birds who will also home. Just one more example of Nature's infinite mystery."

"It seems strange to me that Papa became so fanatical about pigeons, almost to the exclusion of his family."

"You are thinking of that missed Season," he said, and he was correct. The old resentment still lingered.

But I did not wish to speak of it. "It is rather an odd hobby, is it not?" I said instead.

"If that is so, then I am the wrong person to ask. I share his oddity, as men have for thousands of years. Pigeon breeding goes back to three thousand B.C. If it was good enough for the sultan of Baghdad and Genghis Khan, then it is good enough for me."

"You are putting yourself in poor company with Genghis Khan, Snoad," I laughed.

"True," he agreed, "but *clever* poor company. He

adopted the sultan's system of using pigeons for post, by means of a relay system strung over continents. Your father has some excellent literature on the subject. You will notice that I am trying to interest you in it as well, to convince you to keep up the loft. It really would be a shame to lose your father's years of work and study."

I gave him a pert look. "The possibility that you were trying to cozen me had occurred to me. Do the pigeons make money, or lose it?"

He gave a pausing frown. "In a good year, we break even. It is not a scheme for growing rich, but it won't beggar you either. The major investment of preparing the loft has already been made. It will cost you money to disassemble it. We who indulge in the sport consider it a labor of love. One never counts the financial cost when it is a matter of love." He peered down at me hopefully. "Am I making any headway at all, Miss Hume?"

"I shall think about it, Snoad."

While I would never become so fanatical as Papa, it might be an amusing hobby. Now that I was coming to know Snoad better, I thought he might be an interesting addition to my circle of acquaintances. A person knowledgeable in some new sphere will always amuse us for a while.

We walked along the parapet as we talked, admiring the view. A star-dogged moon floated behind a rag of cloud. The cloud glowed a moment, then the moon reappeared. Two miles to the west, a sprinkle of lights announced the presence of Hythe. We stopped at the potted tree that was at the end of the walk.

"Where is Caesar tonight?" I asked. "I didn't see

him in his tree when I was up this afternoon, and he is not here now."

"Sometimes he nests with Cleo."

"Is she named for Cleopatra, since she is Caesar's mate?"

"Yes, her formal name is Cleopatra, but she does not share her namesake's fickle nature."

"Such a paragon of fidelity ought to be named after Caesar's wife."

"Ah, but which one? He had so many."

"Did he? I thought he was only married to ... Octavia, was it, in Shakespeare's play?"

"Calphurnia, actually. But there were others. Cornelia was his first—she died. Then he took up with a lady called Pompeia. He divorced her. Not all Caesar's wives behaved as Caesar's wife ought. It was she who gave rise to the famous quotation that 'Caesar's wife must be above suspicion.' In any case, your father had a fondness for that charming wench, Cleopatra. Our Cleopatra is true to her Caesar, even when he is away on an extended race."

"Why does Caesar have a tree, when none of the other birds have?"

"Because he wants one, and when you are a Caesar, you get what you want. I believe he has a strain of nutmeg pigeon in him. They are arboreal, and solitary for choice. Caesar gets his large size and stamina from his papa, and his pretty coppery-green feathers and red feet from his mama. She was a Ducula Aenea. They have a pair of offspring, young Sextus and Aurelia. Family names of the Caesars," he added. "Your father hoped to have them officially declared Humes. When a fancier has bred a new strain, he may have it named after him. More than a hundred men have already had the honor.

And also a few ladies, incidentally. The Duchess of Prescott would be angry with me if I neglected to mention her triumph."

This potential honor was quite effective in convincing me to keep the loft. I had no aversion to being in the company of duchesses. "What was she like, the duchess?" I asked, as the chance might never rise again, and I was becoming curious about this lady.

"A hotheaded beauty," he replied, with a fond smile. No doubt he saw the suspicion in my eyes, for he hastened to add, "A great charmer in her day, I believe. She was nudging fifty when I left Wiltshire."

"Why did you leave, Snoad?"

"I had a touch of lung trouble. The doctor recommended sea air. The duchess had heard of your father's flock, and recommended me to him. And that is the not very exciting story of how I came to Gracefield, to help your father breed Caesar and Cleo."

"Did the duchess have any daughters?" I asked, with an air of casualness.

"Three married daughters, scattered about here and there. Why do you ask?" he said. A smile quirked his lips.

"Idle curiosity."

I had learned what I wished to know. Snoad was not the man to waste his charms on a fifty-year-old lady, and the daughters were not at home. "Do Sextus and Aurelia show promise?"

"Sextus promises to outperform his father. Aurelia, we felt, would be used for further breeding. From both appearance and performance, I expect your father would have succeeded in establishing his own strain."

"Well, I shall think about keeping the birds, Snoad. I enjoyed our visit."

"I hope you will come again soon, Miss Hume." His hand made an involuntary move toward mine. He stopped it before our hands touched, but we were both conscious of the gesture. It lent an air of embarrassment to our parting.

"I shall be away for a few days, as you know," I mentioned.

"Yes—about that visit. Remember what I said. Be careful."

"What do you think might happen?"

He studied me a moment before speaking. "I don't know. I only know your father was murdered, and now you are going to the same place where he was killed. Until we learn why he was shot, I am concerned for your safety."

"It is very unsettling," I said. Then before either of us said more, I removed his coat, and left.

Snoad watched me go. "Thank you for the watch, Miss Hume," he called after me.

"You're welcome. Good night, Mr. Snoad."

It was not until I was downstairs that I noticed I had called him Mr. Snoad. Whatever possessed me to give him the dignity of that "Mr.," when I had been calling him Snoad for years? It was his conversation, so surprisingly cultured. Who would have thought Snoad knew about Julius Caesar, and Shakespeare? He spoke like an educated man. I found myself wondering how he had been treated at Branksome Hall. I also searched my mind in vain for any mention of lung trouble when he first came to us.

The duchess thought highly enough of him to give him a gold watch, so there could be no scandal with her daughters. He was not what I thought he would be like at all. He was better-spoken, friendlier, more ... thoughtful, really quite nice. But dangerously handsome. I had underestimated his appeal. He was one of those people who improve on longer acquaintance. There would be no disgraceful scandal over the mistress of the house carrying on with a servant at Gracefield.

Chapter Four

Aunt Lovatt and I were relieved to see the weather was fine for our trip the next morning. The only regret was that I did not have proper mourning attire. I had outgrown the clothes from my mother's mourning. The modiste had hastily fashioned one black gown for me, but it was a gown for evening. My pelisse was pale blue. Mrs. Lovatt decided that my navy traveling suit and navy straw bonnet with the flowers removed would be more fitting. They made me look like a governess, but I wore them. Mrs. Lovatt was better equipped. She, at least, would be wearing somber black.

Bunny Smythe posted over at eight-thirty, as promised. His mourning attire was limited to a black arm band and a black ribbon around his hat. Even in our well-sprung carriage, a journey of over fifty miles was no small undertaking. The road along the sea was well maintained and well traveled, however. Between the natural beauty of the coast and the diversion provided by many towns and villages, we were kept from brooding on the troublesome nature of our quest. After a stop for lunch at Eastbourne, we arrived at Brighton in midafternoon.

Both its charms and geography were familiar to us. Brighton was a favorite spot for a weekend's vacation from Hythe. The Prince of Wales's Pavilion had made it a mecca for holidayers of the nobility, and for the commoners who came to gawk at their antics. It was not the onion domes of the Royal Pavilion that drew our interest that day, but the Royal Crescent Hotel at the east end of town, just off the Marine Parade.

"We shall try if we can to get the same room Papa had," I said as we approached the portals.

"The room will have been cleaned; you will not find any clues, if that is what you mean," Mrs. Lovatt replied.

Still, it was worth a try. We were left cooling our heels at the desk. I put the time to good use to scan the registry. A lump formed in my throat when I saw Papa's name, inscribed in his familiar crabbed script. *Harold Hume Esq., Gracefield, Hythe*, it said. He was registered in the Prince George Suite. If the suite lived up to its name, it would be the most lavish set of rooms in the hotel. Such lordly accommodations did not sound like my father's way of carrying on.

"We would like the Prince George Suite," I announced when the clerk attended us. He was a pompous-looking little dandy, of the sort commonly called a "man milliner."

He looked from me to Mrs. Lovatt, and over our shoulders to Bunny Smythe. "Is it a honeymoon, ma'am?" he asked. Mrs. Lovatt's inclusion in the party confused him.

"No, it is Mrs. Lovatt and myself who wish the Prince George," I said.

"That suite is often used by honeymooners." He glanced at some papers beside the registry and said, "Unfortunately, that suite is spoken for. Lord Fairfield will be arriving any moment."

"Oh dear, and I did so want to see Papa's room," I said to Auntie. "Would it be possible for us to just see it?" I asked the clerk. "My father was Mr. Harold Hume," I added in an undertone, thinking the name would be familiar to him. A death at the hotel must have caused quite a ruckus.

He recognized the name at once. "A most tragic and regrettable accident," he said. "I can show you the suite, if you would like a quick glance at it."

"Yes, we would."

"I can give you and Mrs. Lovatt the Eastview Room," he suggested, and mentioned the lovely view from the window. We signed up for this chamber, and Bunny took a room on the west side with a promised view of the Royal Crescent.

The clerk, whose name was Mr. Soames, personally escorted us to the Prince George Suite. "Here we are," he said, throwing the door open to a view of unaccustomed splendor. The gleam of gilt and glare of red canopy and window hangings struck the eye with a blinding force.

"Are you quite sure Mr. Hume stayed here?" Mrs. Lovatt asked in a weak voice.

"Yes indeed, ma'am. Mr. Hume always stayed in the best suite. I'll just leave you to have a look around. But I should remind you, Lord Fairfield will be arriving shortly." He bowed and left.

"Before you leave us, Mr. Soames," I said, "could you tell us anything about my father's death? How it came about, or when it happened. We were quite at a loss when we learned he was shot, for we had been told it was a heart attack."

"Oh dear!" he said, with a worried look. "Oh dear. Shot—yes, we thought it was a water jar falling. Just at the supper hour it happened, when most of the rooms were empty."

"Did he have any visitors?"

"No, none. He had been out that afternoon, and returned to change for dinner. Perhaps someone was with him. We are busy here, you know. We cannot keep an eye on everyone who comes into the hotel. We are all deeply sorry, Miss Hume." He continued on a tide of condolences as he backed away. He was so flustered that I took pity on the man and let him escape.

We walked into the suite, staring and blinking in astonishment. "There is some mistake. Harold never stayed in this room," Mrs. Lovatt declared.

Bunny had strolled to the bed and was lifting the skirt to peer under it. I went to the desk and began opening drawers to search for clues. It was Mrs. Lovatt who discovered the adjoining saloon. It was rigged up like a polite saloon, with sofas, tables, chairs, and pictures on the wall. When I joined her, she said, "Unless your papa held some important meetings here, I cannot imagine what he would want with this extravagance. It would cost a fortune."

"It's just as well we aren't hiring it," I said in a small voice. I had been going over my father's bankbook when his estate was being wound up. He had not taken any very large sums from the bank prior to his trips to London—or Brighton. Soames had mentioned Papa "always" hired this lavish suite. Had he been coming here all along?

"Found something!" Bunny called in an excited tone.

We raced in to find him kneeling by the bed, holding a feather. "This was under the bed," he announced.

"Good gracious," Mrs. Lovatt laughed. "He would not have brought the birds here. He would have left the cage in the stable. That is a goose feather, from a feather duster."

Bunny pocketed the feather and we continued our search. The rooms revealed no further clues. We were about to give up and leave when the door flew open and a young gentleman stepped in. He stopped dead in his tracks and stared at us. His eyes, of a brilliant cerulean blue, studied us each in turn, finally settling on me. "You must be Miss Hume," he said, in a cultured voice.

"Yes, and you, I collect, are Lord Fairfield. I am sorry. We are just leaving."

"The clerk explained that I might find you here—and the reason. May I express my condolences on your loss, Miss Hume. Please, take your time. I shall return later."

While he spoke, I subjected the newcomer to a thorough examination, and decided he belonged on a pedestal in Greece. From the tip of his sleek golden head to the toe of his shining Hessians, and in every inch of the intervening six feet, he was perfection. His noble visage might have been chiseled by Pericles. His body, while somewhat slighter than the Greek ideal, was perfectly proportioned.

I pulled myself back to attention and replied, "We

were just leaving, milord. I am sorry to have intruded."

"On the contrary! It is I who feel an intruder. You must have this suite. We shall exchange."

"Oh no! Really, that is not at all necessary. We only wanted to see it."

"I insist!"

Mrs. Lovatt advanced to introduce herself and Mr. Smythe, as I had lost all sense of propriety. "Very kind of you, sir, but we do not require such a lavish set of rooms."

"Nor do I!" he insisted.

"But we don't want it, milord!" I assured him.

"We cannot afford it," Mrs. Lovatt added bluntly, as her concern for the gentleman's good opinion did not quite match mine.

"I shall arrange the matter to your satisfaction," he said, and left, his ears still ringing with denials.

"What a pickle!" I complained. "You need not have told him we couldn't afford it, Auntie. He was just trying to be civil."

"Daresay he didn't want it himself, once he got a look at it," Bunny said.

We were still discussing the vexing situation a moment later when our bags were brought up by a hotel page, accompanied by the pompous little clerk. I used the word "little" in the sense of insignificant. Soames was tall as a bean pole, and of roughly similar width.

"Lord Fairfield insists you have his suite. There will be no change in the price of your accommodation," Soames said discreetly.

"We don't want him to pay for us," I exclaimed.

"The hotel is happy to defray the cost, madam,

as a token of our esteem for your late father's patronage."

"In that case, I hope you will thank Lord Fairfield for us. And thank you, sir," Mrs. Lovatt said.

Satisfied smiles were exchanged all around. Even Mrs. Lovatt was content with the arrangement. We were both fully alive to the glories of the suite, and particularly to the benefit of getting it at a nominal cost. She allowed it was "very handsome" of both Lord Fairfield and the hotel to take this generous stand. Bunny Smythe went to his room, promising to return shortly.

"We shall write up some notices for the Brighton journals, Heather, inquiring for information of your father, and have them delivered at once," Mrs. Lovatt said. "I'll include the word 'urgent.' If they appear in tomorrow's papers, we shall not have to stay longer than two days."

"I wonder how long Lord Fairfield is remaining in town," I said, smiling vaguely at the doorway that had taken my hero away.

"He didn't say. I wonder if we ought to write him a note and thank him," Auntie said, striding purposefully to the desk. She drew out the cream vellum paper. "This stationery looks almost too good to use for the notices."

I helped myself to a sheet. "It will do nicely for my note to Lord Fairfield."

While I struggled over making a three-line note to Lord Fairfield a thing of beauty, Mrs. Lovatt wrote and sealed notices to the three Brighton journals. Mr. Smythe returned as we were sealing our respective missives.

"No need for us to deliver them. The hotel will have them taken around," he informed us.

"Excellent, then that leaves us free to have a nice cup of tea," Mrs. Lovatt said. "My head is splitting after our long drive. We'll have it in the saloon. That saloon will come in handy if we actually get any replies to those notices. We cannot interview strangers in the bedroom, and the lobby would not give us any privacy."

She pulled the bell chord, sent off the various letters, and ordered tea. When we were comfortable in the saloon with tea poured and a plate of sandwiches before us, we got down to discussing our unhappy business.

"The next step is to visit a constable and show him the bullet holes in Papa's jacket," I said.

"I'll handle that," Bunny said. "No need for you ladies to be put upon. I'll find out which officer handled the case and give him a stiff quizzing. Seems to me there ought to have been some clues. Mean to say, you don't shoot a fellow in a high-class hotel like this without attracting some attention. And some blood," he added, peering down at the striped sofa.

I stiffened, and began to look around the carpet and sofa.

"I already checked," Mrs. Lovatt said. "If it happened in this room, the hotel has cleared away all signs. You might ask that nice, friendly clerk exactly where it happened, Mr. Smythe."

"I'll have a word with him, too." He lifted a ham sandwich, frowned at it, then returned it to his plate. All this talk of blood had taken away everyone's appetite for meat. He reached for a slice of cream cake instead. Two slices later, he was just rising to leave when there was a tap on the door.

An image of Lord Fairfield leapt into my head. I

made an unladylike bolt for the door. A shy smile sat on my lips as I drew it open. The smile faded to a question at the first view of the caller. He was as insignificant and uninteresting as Lord Fairfield was outstanding and memorable. The man was of medium height, pale of face, with straight brown hair and hazel eyes. He was outfitted like a gentleman in a decent blue jacket and faun trousers, but one looked in vain for any elegance or charm. Stick a pencil behind his ear, and he might be a junior clerk from any place of business.

"Miss Hume?" he asked, in a flat voice.

"I am Miss Hume."

"Depew," he said, handing me a card. I glanced at it and read *Sir Chauncey Depew, K.B.E.* The name meant nothing to me, but my lively imagination soon suggested that Lord Fairfield was involved.

"Might I have a word with you?" He looked up and down the hall, as if afraid of being overheard.

"Certainly," I said, and stood aside to let him enter.

"I have come about your father's death," he announced.

"Pray come into the saloon, Sir Chauncey." He looked taken aback to see I had company. "This is my aunt, Mrs. Lovatt. Mr. Hume's sister," I explained. "And this is my cousin, Mr. Smythe."

Bunny narrowed his eyes in suspicion. Sir Chauncey bowed. He looked unhappily at Smythe. "This is a private matter," he said to me, *sotto voce*.

"Mr. Smythe is here for the purpose of helping me look into Papa's death. You can count on his discretion," I said.

"Mum's the word," Bunny said, tapping his nose.

Sir Chauncey was given a seat. He looked around nervously, moistened his lips, and said, "An extremely distressing business. My first duty is to tender my condolences. An extremely regrettable affair."

"Thank you," I said dutifully, waiting to hear what more pressing reason had brought him.

"I was to meet your father here the evening he ... passed away."

"Did you meet him?" I demanded. At last, someone who knew what had really happened!

"No, he was gone by the time I arrived."

"Do you mean gone from the premises, or dead?" I asked bluntly.

"Deceased." He could not bring himself to use the common four-letter word.

"What was your business with him, Sir Chauncey?" Mrs. Lovatt asked.

"He was to give me some information—a message," he said vaguely.

"We don't know what you are talking about," I said bluntly. "We have come here to look for information, not give it. Was it something to do with the pigeons?"

"Precisely!" he said, with a significant nod of his head, which meant nothing to any of his auditors.

"You would have to speak to Snoad, my father's helper with his birds, about that. He is at Gracefield," I explained.

"Snoad," Depew said, puzzling over the name. "Were the birds your father brought with him returned to Gracefield then?"

I just stared a moment, thinking. "That is odd! His coffin was returned, and his valise, but what

49

happened to the birds? He usually took a dozen with him."

"They are not here. I inquired," Depew said.

"Was it a particularly valuable bird you were interested in?" Mrs. Lovatt asked.

"Extremely valuable," Depew replied, frowning.

Smythe took no part in the conversation, except to listen and look. What he stared at for the most part was the buttons on Depew's jacket. They were rather ornate, with some sort of crest on them.

Mrs. Lovatt said, "If they are not here, I daresay the hotel got rid of them. They would have starved long since, with no one to feed them."

Depew shook his head. "I inquired the night of your father's demise. The cage was already missing."

I thought it showed a lack of feeling that Depew should have worried about pigeons at such a time, but I knew well enough that Papa was equally obsessed by the birds, and forgave him.

"I am sorry we cannot be of help to you, sir, but if you wish to be in touch with Mr. Snoad, I daresay he could sell you a bird of equal value to the one you wanted to buy. He knows as much about all that business as my father did."

Smythe said, "Was it here you was to meet Mr. Hume, or in London, Sir Chauncey?"

"London?" he asked, startled. "No, it was here. Why should you think it was London?"

"Because my father's coffin was sent from London," I explained. "That is where he told us he was going, to a meeting of the Columbidae Society. It is very odd, is it not?"

Sir Chauncey frowned into his collar. "London! That is odd." He looked as if he would say more, but he came to an abrupt halt. "Are you quite certain?"

"Indeed we are," I assured him. "It is a matter of the utmost confusion to us as well, Sir Chauncey."

"London," he repeated. His shock now held a tinge of something akin to fear.

He drew out his watch and glanced at it. As his jacket moved aside, Smythe peered to check the lining. It was of yellow silk. "I must dash. Snoad, you said, at Gracefield?"

"Yes, Mr. Snoad is tending the pigeons," I assured him.

Depew rose. "Thank you very much, Miss Hume. A pleasure to meet you, ma'am, sir," he added to the others, already hastening to the door.

As there was no hope of catching him, I let him show himself out. "What do you make of that?" I asked Auntie.

"Very mysterious, to be sure. We didn't get much out of him, did we?"

"He knows even less than we do," I replied. "He didn't even know Papa's body was taken to London. He seemed upset to hear it. I wonder why."

"Horse Guards," Smythe announced.

Mrs. Lovatt asked, "What's that you say, Smythe?"

"Depew—he was wearing the prince's buttons on his jacket. Yaller lining as well. He's with the Horse Guards."

"Is he indeed? He did not say so."

"Stands to reason he wouldn't. I wonder he didn't change his jacket to call on you. Course, he didn't know I would be here," he added, to answer his own question. Provincial ladies, I assumed he meant,

51

would not realize the significance of the prince's buttons. Nor did we. The two questioning faces tacitly demanded an explanation. "Thing is," he said, "the man's a spy." Two gasps rent the air. "An English spy," he hastened to assure us. "Horse Guards handle intelligence for the war. Coincidence, I daresay. Your father had nothing to do with the war. Anyone might fancy pigeons; even a spy can have a hobby."

"I thought a spy would be more dashing," I said. An image of Lord Fairfield darted into my head. Somewhere at the back of my mind there lurked an image of Snoad as well, but it was soon overshadowed by my new noble acquaintance. "This becomes more confusing by the moment," I said, and drew a deep sigh. "Let us go out for a breath of air. Is your headache better, Auntie?"

"The tea helped. A breath of air might finish the job. The Royal Pavilion is too far. We'll stroll along the Marine Parade and enjoy the fresh breeze."

"I'll nip along to see the constable," Smythe said.

Aunt Lovatt got him the parcel holding Papa's jacket and shirt. We both donned our pelisses and bonnets. It was as we were leaving that we discovered the key to the suite was not in the room. We had to stop at the desk to get it, and I returned above to lock the door. Bunny also had to inquire at the desk for the route to the constable's office.

Eventually we were all ready to leave. The gusty breeze outside was not only fresh but chilling. A short walk was enough to turn Mrs. Lovatt's headache to a fear of taking a chill. Before we were blown to pieces, we returned at a rapid gait, with the wind pulling at our skirts and bonnets.

"Have a lie-down before dinner, Auntie," I suggested when we recovered the comfort of the hotel. "I'll wait to hear what Bunny learns from the constable."

"I'll do that. And I'll light the fire, too. I noticed it was laid, ready for lighting."

I unlocked the door and we entered by the saloon. It was not until Mrs. Lovatt went into the bedroom that anything irregular was noticed. She called to me in a hollow voice. "Heather, come and have a look at this."

I darted in, thinking to see some clue relating to my father's death. I saw Auntie staring in dismay at our open cases, with our clothes strewn about the room. We were both too shocked to be angry yet. "What on earth happened?"

"We have had a visitor," Mrs. Lovatt said. She began picking up garments and examining them.

"Has anything been stolen?" I demanded, racing for my jewelry box. It contained a string of pearls and a matching ring. The box had been opened, but both were intact. Mrs. Lovatt had not brought any jewelry.

"An odd sort of thief. He didn't take anything," I said. "Should we report it to the desk?"

Mrs. Lovatt sank on the side of the bed to collect her wits. "I dread to do it, we've been such a nuisance to that nice man already."

"I think we must. The door had not been pried open. In fact, it was locked when we returned. Someone besides us has a key."

"Lord Fairfield!" Mrs. Lovatt exclaimed. "He would have been given a key when he hired the room."

"You cannot think he would have done this!" I scoffed.

"Someone did it. Why did he want your father's room in the first place?"

"He just wanted the best rooms the hotel had. I'll ring for Soames," I said. I didn't believe for a moment that Lord Fairfield would be so savage as to have done this foul deed. It seemed to me more like the work of the mysterious Sir Chauncey Depew. Obviously it had something to do with Papa's death.

Chapter Five

In five minutes Soames was at the door. "Lord Fairfield's valet turned their key in at the desk before you left for your walk, Miss Hume," he told me when I put the question to him. "I hope there has not been any more ... trouble?" he asked, sniffing the air for gunpowder.

"Someone entered while we were out. I feel he used a key, as the lock is not damaged."

His white brow pleated in concern. "There is one key missing," he said. "Your father's. The hotel never recovered it."

"Then it stands to reason whoever killed Papa has the key, and came to search our belongings."

"This is a fine how-do-you-do," Mrs. Lovatt declared, tossing up her hands in despair. "We might be shot in the back like your father before the night is over. We must change rooms at once."

Soames had a small fit of hysterics. I cannot imagine why he was so eager for our troublesome patronage. He promised to have the locks changed immediately. He was very sorry for our inconvenience. In fact, he said we might stay as long as we wished at no expense. But only for three days, as Lady Eileen somebody had hired the suite for that date.

A free suite was not despised by Mrs. Lovatt, nor by myself. She allowed herself to be talked into remaining. Soames left, and while Auntie and I were still discussing the matter, Bunny Smythe returned bearing his bundle, and wearing an expression of complete mystification.

"What did you learn?" I asked eagerly.

"Demmed odd," he said, shaking his head. "The constable had no notion of any trouble at the Royal Crescent. The murder was never reported."

"Not reported!" I gasped. "But that is impossible! How can we hope to catch the villain if the police don't even know the murder took place?"

"Demmed odd," Bunny repeated. "I had a word with Soames when I came in. Asked why he didn't report it. Orders from Whitehall, he said. There was an officer from the Horse Guards here. He wanted the whole thing hushed up. Depew, obviously."

I just stared at him in disbelief. Poor Bunny had made a botch of it. "What on earth had Papa to do with the Horse Guards?"

"He had something to do with them right enough. I had to get a tad rusty with Soames, but I learned something else as well. Your father wasn't paying for his own accommodations. The order for the room and the money in cash both came from London. Explains why he had such a gaudy suite. Mean to say—he wasn't footing the bill."

My mouth felt dry. This talk of the Horse Guards and letters from London reeled around in my brain.

"Are you saying Papa was a spy, Bunny?" Bad enough that spies were such boring creatures as Depew. Now it seemed my own father was one of them.

"I'm not saying he was a spy. Not saying he wasn't. Just saying he didn't pay for his own rooms, and the Horse Guards took a keen interest in his doings."

"I don't see why they would, unless he was helping them."

"No more do I," he allowed. "Gracefield is a good spot to spy from. Right on the coast. Dover, just a few miles north, is a regular den of spies and smugglers."

The English had no need for information of doings at Hythe, however. They already knew what troops and ships were standing by in case of invasion by Bonaparte's troops. I soon discovered a less flattering reason for the interest of the Horse Guards. Was it possible Papa was a spy for the Frenchies? Anyone could have arranged for the suite from London. I could not believe it. "Why remove his body to London?" I asked.

"And why did someone steal his pigeon cages?" Bunny added. "Seems to me they was all looking for something. Don't see why they couldn't look for it here. Unless they was trying to hush the whole thing up."

"It almost seems it is us they were trying to fool," I said angrily. "They had Papa tell us he was going to London. Perhaps that is why they took his body there, to get the death certificate signed by a London doctor, and have a London firm deliver the body home, pretending he died of a heart attack. We never would have tumbled to it if it were not for

57

receiving Papa's case from the hotel here. That is where the Horse Guards slipped up."

"The hotel slipped up," Bunny said. "Hotel was told to tidy things up, pack the duds, and forward 'em to London. Some junior clerk who didn't know the ins and outs of it exceeded his office. He checked to see where Mr. Hume was from, and thought there was some mistake, so he sent the clothes to Gracefield. Fat was in the fire. Shirt and jacket riddled with bullet holes. *Ipso* after the *facto*, he was shot. No point denying your father was here."

"That must be illegal! Lying to us, and conniving to conceal evidence from the police."

"Plain as the nose on your face they've been lying through their teeth with all this going on behind our backs."

When I had sorted out this anatomical jungle, I agreed.

"Soames says the Horse Guards was furious," Bunny said.

"I expect it is Sir Chauncey Depew who was in charge," I decided. "He didn't seem that bright to me."

"Close as an oyster," Bunny averred. "Not to say he ain't sharp as a tack. They choose those invisible fellows on purpose so you won't notice them. I mentioned Depew to Soames. He didn't recognize him—not the chap who ordered Hume's body shipped to London, he says. Not that I believe him."

"We ought to have a word with Depew, and make him tell us what is going on," Mrs. Lovatt said, with a commanding eye at Bunny.

Smythe agreed to go below and learn what room Depew had taken. He returned in a moment with another unsatisfactory message. "Depew ain't staying at the hotel. Might be putting up elsewhere in Brighton, or might be going back to London. Point non plus—for the nonce. Could always write him a letter."

"I was never so vexed in my life," I declared. "What should we do?"

"I could ankle along to a few other hotels and see if I can find him," Smythe offered.

"Such a lot of unpleasant chores we are saddling you with, Bunny."

"A pleasure," he said gamely, and straggled up from his chair to brave the winds once more.

Mrs. Lovatt and I exchanged a questioning, lost look. "I feel as if I had fallen into a penny novel," I said.

My aunt was silent a moment, thinking. At length, she spoke. "I don't believe a word of all these marvelous tales. Harold was no more a spy than I am."

"How can you not believe, with all the bizarre things that are going on?"

"I don't like to be the one to disillusion you, Heather, but the fact is, Mrs. Mobley lives in Brighton."

"Surely she went to Ireland!"

"Oh yes, she went to Ireland, and remained all of a month. She found it too quiet. I heard the whole story from Mrs. Gibbons, who had it of Mrs. Mobley's brother's cook. I never told Harold. You may imagine why. It seems he found out by himself."

"He would never go back to her after she killed Mama," I exclaimed.

"Don't be a goose. That had nothing to do with your mother's death. If he would see her while his wife was alive, there is no reason to stick at seeing her after she was dead, and he was alone."

"He was not alone! He had us."

"And Snoad," she added angrily.

"He showed extremely poor taste in his choice of the 'other woman.' And this is where she ended up, in Brighton?"

"I wish she had stayed in Ireland, as she was supposed to. Her being here would explain this ludicrous set of rooms Harold hired. Just what that Mobley creature would like."

"It doesn't explain why the Horse Guards or anyone else should pay for the rooms."

"We have only a hotel clerk's word for that. They lied to us about everything else. Soames is trying to wrap the mess up in clean linen, to save your feelings," my aunt decided.

I just looked at her. "If Papa was a spy for his country, it is hardly a case of dirty linen, Auntie. Remember, the Horse Guards took Papa's body to London."

"But was it for *his* country, or for the French?" she asked, in a rhetorical spirit. I was dreadfully depressed to hear her state my own worst fear aloud. "I don't say your father was guilty. I believe he was Snoad's dupe. That is what *I* think."

"Surely not! Snoad was devoted to Papa." Yet I had never thought so until last night, when Snoad had changed his whole personality so drastically that he had seemed a different man entirely. Had he done it to cozen me?

"Before you call me a fool, stop and think a minute," my aunt continued. "When did your father's interest in pigeons run out of all control? When Snoad moved in. Before that, it was just a little hobby. Once Snoad took over, your father suddenly began receiving all manner of strange callers. It was Snoad who arranged for customers, you must know."

"He told me he didn't know who Papa was coming to see in Brighton!"

"Of course he told you that, ninny. Now that he's managed to get your father killed, he wants to distance himself from the business. Birds were always arriving and leaving at a great rate once Snoad moved in. He was using Harold's racers to deliver messages across the Channel to France. The birds delivered to the loft by those strange callers would be from France, to return bearing information. Snoad would keep an eye on the coast, and send back word of what troops were building up. We have any number of military bases in the neighborhood. The Gracefield birds the Frenchies took away would be sent back with requests for what information they required."

"But if Papa only came to Brighton to visit Mrs. Mobley . . . and why should the Horse Guards pay for his rooms?" I asked, trying to make sense of the senseless.

"We don't know that they did. Someone paid by cash enclosed in a letter, is what Soames said. It could have been the Frenchies. Don't think there aren't Frenchies in London."

"Why did Papa bring pigeons then, and why was he killed? He always told us he was going to his Pigeon Society meetings in London."

"Aye, but where he was coming was to Brighton. He discovered in some manner that Mobley was here. She wrote him, no doubt. The pigeon meetings were his pretext to get away and visit Mobley.

He knew I would have something to say if I learned he was seeing that creature. I daresay Snoad just took advantage of the visits. He would be happy enough to have Harold do some of the business away from home. It diverted suspicion from himself—from Snoad I mean. Snoad might have been concealing messages in with the birds in some manner. If the Horse Guards caught on to it, they would have assumed your father was the culprit, and had him assassinated."

"I hope Bunny finds Depew, for there are a *dozen* questions I want to ask him," I said, trying to figure out if my aunt had solved the case, or only complicated it further. Depew was the one who could tell us whether Papa was spying for England, or against it.

"I almost hope he does not," Mrs. Lovatt said. "As things stand, we have only questions to worry us."

"I should prefer to have those questions answered, Auntie. Papa must have wondered why he was getting his room free."

Mrs. Lovatt made no reply, but her worried frown suggested that she was pondering the possibility of Papa's deeper involvement in the spying scheme. After a long moment she said, "Harold always had a reckless streak in him. He was used to letting the smugglers land at his cove. It worried your mama to death."

And smugglers from France, presumably, might easily provide a line to French spies. Snoad had a foreign air about him. Not in his speech, but his coloring was Gallic. Was there not a sort of French passion in his talk of the pigeons the other night as well? We English are more phlegmatic.

We were interrupted by a discreet tap at the door. I felt as if a murderer might be standing outside, ready to pounce in and shoot us. My aunt admitted the caller. My spirits soared to hear the polite accents of Lord Fairfield.

He entered smiling. His eyes swerved at once in my direction, where they seemed to find considerable pleasure. "I hope I am not intruding, ma'am," he said, with an exquisite bow.

"Not at all. Pray have a seat, milord."

He waited until Mrs. Lovatt was seated before taking a chair himself. "Mr. Soames has just been telling me the shocking news of your room being broken into. I came to assure myself you are unharmed," he said. Using this excuse, his darting eyes examined me minutely. His especial concern appeared to focus on my bosom and ankles.

"Indeed we are fine," I assured him. "We were out at the time, and did not discover the break-in until our return."

"My valet took the key down as soon as I left you. No doubt someone picked it up from the desk and came to see if he might find a purse or jewelry lying about."

"If that was his aim, he was disappointed," Mrs. Lovatt replied, pretending to accept this faradiddle.

Regarding Lord Fairfield, I was much struck with his noble mien and broad shoulders. Such a gentleman, from the highest walk of life, would have access to information that was denied ladies of mere gentility. I felt a strong urge to throw all my troubles on his shoulders and ask his help. If there lurked at the back of my mind that a damsel in distress customarily won a proposal from her savior, I did not acknowledge it at the time, even to myself.

When Lord Fairfield inclined his head toward me and said, in a very concerned way, "Is something troubling you, ma'am? You look worried," I was within amesace of opening my budget to him.

Auntie, perhaps sensing my mood, said, "We are just tired from the trip, milord."

He rose at once. "It is unconscionable of me to be imposing on you at this time. There is a matter I wished to discuss with you, but it must wait till later."

No sane possibility of what this matter could be occurred to me, but I said, "I am not at all tired."

Lord Fairfield had just resumed his seat and adjusted his body to a comfortable position in the chair when another tap came at the door. "That will be Smythe," Mrs. Lovatt said, and rose to admit him.

Her sharp intake of breath was audible across the room, but it was soon overborne by the loud and common accents of a female. "G'day, Mrs. Lovatt. I spotted you on the Marine Parade a short while ago and saw you enter the hotel. I have come to pay my condolences on Harold's death."

Lord Fairfield blinked in astonishment at the apparition who elbowed Mrs. Lovatt aside and strode into the chamber, amidst a reek of toilet water. She was a full-blown blond woman of heroic proportions. Her natural color was assisted by a generous application from the rouge pot. She was outfitted all in violet, from the swirling feathers of her high poke bonnet to the tips of her kidskin gloves and kid slippers. If this liberal use of violet was meant to indicate half mourning, it failed miserably. She looked like an actress decked out for a mourning scene, whose performance she was enjoying immensely.

"Such a shock for you, Miss Hume," she said, rushing up to me. "Happening away from home and all, and under such queer circumstances. You must have wondered what had hit you." As she spoke, her eyes flashed with keen interest toward Lord Fairfield.

I was obliged to perform the introduction. "Lord Fairfield, this is an old neighbor from Hythe, Mrs. Mobley."

"Not that old!" Mrs. Mobley assured him, with a playful nudge and something dangerously close to a wink.

Fairfield had risen to his feet upon her entrance. He made a very civil bow, and said, "Charmed, madam."

Mrs. Mobley, with a deal of commotion, arranged her reticule, umbrella, and a bag of something she had been carrying on the table beside her. She then turned to me. "Have you found out what carried off your father?" she demanded, with the avid eagerness of the born gossip.

I was acutely aware of Lord Fairfield's eyes upon me. I was glad Mrs. Mobley didn't know Papa had been shot. It seemed a vulgar way to die. "That is why we have come, but we have not learned anything yet. And how are you liking Brighton, Mrs. Mobley?" I asked hastily, hoping to divert the conversation to harmless topics. "I heard you had gone to Ireland."

"Ireland is a wonderful climate—for potatoes," she said. "I stuck it out for as long as I could. I much prefer Brighton. It's lively. It is. Between Prinney's visits and bathing and boating, and of course, your father's visits, I have been well entertained."

Mrs. Lovatt's spine stiffened, as if a poker had suddenly been inserted up it. "I had not realized you were on terms with the Prince Regent," she said, with awful irony.

Mrs. Mobley emitted a raucous bark of laughter. "Good gracious, Mrs. Lovatt, I have not *met* him. I simply meant it is good fun to watch the old walrus carrying his belly along the streets. Mind you, I have not entirely given up on scraping an acquaintance, for he is partial to mature ladies, and has no love of string beans." A condemning eye raked Mrs. Lovatt's ladderlike frame. "When a lady reaches our age, she must give up on either her face or her figure. If you try to lose a pound, the first place it goes is the face."

"Your face has certainly not lost its bloom," Mrs. Lovatt retorted, staring at the rolls of fat around the lady's middle.

"Harold thought I was just the right size." She smiled. "Speaking of Harold, I daresay it was his heart that carried him off?"

"Yes," Mrs. Lovatt replied, with a warning glance in my direction.

"He mentioned those palpitations when we were—" She came to a coy pause, and smiled at Lord Fairfield. "When we were engaging in any strenuous activity."

"He found walking fatiguing," Mrs. Lovatt said, her voice like ice. "You ought not to have let him exert himself, Mrs. Mobley."

"Try if you could stop him!" she said, and laughed merrily. Her next embarrassments were directed to Lord Fairfield, from whom she hoped to obtain an invitation to the Royal Pavilion. "As you are a fine lord, I daresay you are putting up at Prinney's place?" she asked.

"I am staying here at the Royal Crescent," he answered civilly.

"Just a social visit? Will you be visiting the prince?"

"I am here on business, actually."

"Feel free to call on me, if you have an hour at your disposal. I live on German Street, just off the Marine Parade. A tidy little red cottage. You'll know it by the daffodils around the gate. I'm sure any friends of the Humes are friends of mine."

Mrs. Lovatt bridled in frustration at this impertinence.

"You are very kind," he said, trying to conceal his astonishment. Then he rose. "I know you ladies are tired, so I shan't trouble you further. May I return later this evening to discuss that matter I mentioned, ladies?"

"We plan to return to our room immediately after dinner," I replied.

"I look forward to seeing you then." He bowed all around, and left.

"A new beau, Miss Hume?" Mrs. Mobley asked.

"I only met Lord Fairfield today."

"But your papa knew him," the dame said knowingly.

"I don't believe so."

"I'm sure I've seen him chatting to Harold, though I was never presented to him before. They exchanged letters once, I think. Harold used to meet an odd assortment of men. When was it now?" She gave a frowning pause. "Yes, it was during Harold's Christmas visit that I spotted his lordship. We had been shopping—Harold bought that dainty little gold locket for you, Miss Hume. We stopped here at the hotel for tea. Harold excused himself and had a word with Fairfield. He didn't mention the lad's name, but I am not likely to forget a face like that. Handsome as can stare."

I was on thorns to learn how Papa had known Lord Fairfield, and was aware, too, of her confirmation that Papa had indeed been coming to Brighton all along. Mrs. Mobley could not know he had given me that little gold locket at Christmas unless she had been with my father when he bought it. I was incensed to realize that Papa had been pulling the wool over our eyes, and with this ill-bred creature.

"And what did he buy for you, Mrs. Mobley?" Mrs. Lovatt asked, in a sharp tone.

"Not a wedding ring, if that is what's got your back up. Marriage didn't suit me, though we discussed it. He could not leave Gracefield, and I had no wish to go there." Her gimlet gaze said as clear as words who it was she objected to.

"It is strange Papa never mentioned Lord Fairfield," I said.

"Aye." Mrs. Mobley nodded sagely. "There were odd things aplenty going on with your father. I don't know what it was; he said it would be safer for me not to know. It was a great secret. One would think he was a spy, the way he carried on," she laughed. "Would you have any notion at all what brought him here, Miss Hume? He'd been coming half a year before I bumped into him."

"It was bird business," Mrs. Lovatt said.

"Still racing his pigeons, was he? That explains all those odd-looking men he used to meet."

"What do you mean?" I demanded.

"Why, you may be sure they were fixing the races. Arranging amongst themselves whose bird was to win, and laying bets on it. That sort of thing goes on all the time. I wish he had told me. I am not a gambler, but I wouldn't have minded picking up a few pounds on a sure thing. But then, we had more interesting things to talk about. Well, I must be trotting along. I just wanted to pay my respects. Nice chatting to you again."

Not a word was said to detain her. She heaved herself from her chair, assembled her belongings, and I showed her to the door, with a few insincere expressions of gratitude.

"Hussy!" Mrs. Lovatt exclaimed when the door was closed. "Wouldn't you know she would have to land in when Lord Fairfield was here. What must he think of that creature? At least she didn't mention her suspicion that Harold was a spy." She stopped and emitted a gasp. "Good gracious, Heather. Do you think Mrs. Mobley could be in on it?"

"She'd have been boasting of it if she were. What do you think of this idea of fixing the races, Auntie?"

"Your father was a gentleman, miss."

"Then I fear he was a gentleman spy. It is odd, her eagerness to get to the Royal Pavilion. That would be an excellent place to pick up news."

"Yes," Mrs. Lovatt said doubtfully, "though I can easily enough believe it is the prince she wishes to pick up there. Thank God at least Harold didn't marry her. She has an eye for Fairfield, you must have noticed."

I laughed. "She is a bit long in the tooth for him."

"And a bit broad in the beam."

"I shall ask him this evening how he came to know Papa."

"I am beginning to think we should drop this entire matter," my aunt said. "Whatever it is, it's over and done now."

"Not really," I said. "If it was Snoad at the bottom of it, as you think, then it might be still going on."

It was unusual for Mrs. Lovatt to have overlooked this aspect of it, for in the usual way, she is awake on all suits. "We'll march Snoad out of Gracefield as soon as we get home."

I was aware of a strange reluctance. I remembered Snoad's sadness when he spoke of my father, and his emotion when I had given him the watch. He had looked so very handsome in the moonlight. . . .

Chapter Six

We did not see Bunny Smythe again until dinnertime. He sent a note to our room telling us he had hired a private parlor, and would meet us there.

"I ordered wine and was just having a gargle," he said, rising to greet us when we entered. "More than ready for fork work after a busy day. Look forward to sinking a bicuspid into a piece of red meat."

He had changed to evening attire, but there is not a jacket in all of Christendom that can make Bunny look elegant. Black, in particular, did not suit him. He had the uncanny faculty of attracting every mote of dust and hair and dirt in the air. His jacket looked for the world like a dust rag. He looks least bad in country jacket, buckskins, and top boots. In evening clothes, he looked like a hired mourner at a second-rate funeral.

As soon as we were seated and given a glass of wine to await our mutton, I said, "Did you have any luck finding Depew?"

"Not a sniff of him. He isn't putting up at any of the regular hotels. Plenty of rooming houses, of course."

"I don't see Sir Chauncey putting up at a rooming house," Mrs. Lovatt said.

"Might, if his visit is supposed to be a secret."

We filled Bunny in on our doings during his absence. No mention was made of the possibility of Papa's involvement in spying being anything but proper. "So this is where Mrs. Mobley has anchored herself," he said.

"Do you know anything about Lord Fairfield?" I asked. Bunny made occasional darts to London during the Season, and had friends there from his school days, and his one term at Cambridge.

"Bit of a wild buck. Corinthian—baron. Heir to old Lord Albemarle's title and estates. One in Hampshire, another up north somewhere. Marquess, the papa. Fairfield'll be rich as Croesus one day. Meanwhile, he's usually dipped. Bets on the horses."

"Perhaps he also bets on the pigeon races," I said. "I cannot think what else he would be doing with Papa."

"Never heard of a Corinthian betting on pigeons," Bunny said. "Though now you mention it, they do sometimes bet on pigs and dogs and whatnot. Bet on anything, really. Thing to do, ask him tonight when he calls. You said he was calling?"

"Yes," I replied, with a conscious smile.

"Flies too high for you, m'dear," Bunny warned. "Regular dasher. Top o' the trees. Higher."

Far from depressing my intention, this only pushed Lord Fairfield closer to the sun, and increased my desire to attach him. The mutton arrived and was consumed with some pleasure. As we sipped our tea, I said, "I wonder what time Lord Fairfield will call. Perhaps we ought to go upstairs now. We would not want to keep him waiting."

Mrs. Lovatt abetted me in this notion. We had often discussed the dearth of good partis at Hythe. We had no objection to a gambling man, so long as he could afford his pleasure, and Lord Fairfield obviously could count on his father to foot any little overdrafts he might accumulate.

After running upstairs with our dinner still in our throats, we waited a full hour for Fairfield's tap at the door. When he came, he was thought well worth the wait. Unlike Bunny, he looked stunning in his evening clothes. They fit so well, they might have grown on him. The dramatic black outfit was enhanced by his white cravat, his high coloring, and the brilliancy of his blue eyes.

As he made his bows, I wondered which seat he would take. When he walked to the sofa and sat beside me, I felt flustered, and insensibly pleased.

"What was the matter you wished to discuss, Lord Fairfield?" I asked, after a few civilities had been exchanged.

"I share your late father's fascination with pigeon racing," he said, with a somewhat embarrassed look in Smythe's direction. "Truth to tell, I have come a cropper racing my nags. Pigeons are cheaper. I have heard word along the grapevine that your father had a rare champion, a bird named Caesar, I believe. I do not wish to appear callous, but since your father's demise, I wondered if you were planning to sell off his birds. I should like to make an offer on Caesar and Cleo, and perhaps some of the others."

"So that is how you met Papa!" I exclaimed.

"Met him?" he asked in surprise.

"Mrs. Mobley mentioned she had seen you with him, right here at this hotel."

He frowned a moment, then seemed to recall. "It is true, I did once approach him last winter. I introduced myself as a fellow racer, but he was rather busy at the time. We just exchanged cards. Your father said he would be in touch, but he never contacted me. I did not like to put myself forward with the country's most renowned breeder."

It seemed incredible that Lord Fairfield should be shy of putting himself forward anywhere, but I was flattered that he had so much respect for Papa. "I do plan to sell the whole roost," I said, "but the pigeons are trained like homing pigeons, to return to Gracefield. What use would they be to you, milord?" I had not actually *promised* Snoad to keep the pigeons.

He hesitated a moment, then said, "For breeding. It seems a shame to let those two prodigies die out. I expect you will have any number of buyers after them. What price are you asking for them?"

"Snoad would be the one to give us the price. He runs the roost," I explained.

"Snoad?" he asked, his brows raised in question.

"Snoad is the man who helped Papa train his birds. He is very knowledgeable, I believe. He used to be with the Duchess of Prescott, at Branksome Hall."

"Trained with the Duchess of Prescott, you say? She certainly has a fine flock. Would it be convenient for me to visit you at Gracefield, after your return?"

"We would be very happy to see you, milord," I said, and could not suppress a smile.

"Has Snoad been with you long?" he asked.

"For two years, more or less."

"He will be leaving us immediately," Mrs. Lovatt added.

"As soon as you disband your flock," he said, nodding. "Naturally someone must be in charge of the birds until that time. It seems a great pity to lose out on all Mr. Hume's work, does it not? Just when he had developed a new strain, too. Caesar's offspring were to be named after your father, I believe? It must grieve you deeply to give them up, Miss Hume."

I heard the echoes of Snoad in this speech, and wondered if I was doing the right thing to so heedlessly toss out my father's work. "Yes, it is a pity," I agreed, "but I know virtually nothing about raising pigeons, or training them."

"Must Snoad leave you?" he asked. "He sounds the proper one to teach you."

I felt guilty, and said vaguely, "Now that my father is gone, Snoad will not remain long."

"I hope we can salvage Caesar and Cleo's strain at least. You may rest assured the Hume strain will be well tended, if I am the fortunate breeder who obtains them."

There was not a single doubt in my mind that Fairfield would be the purchaser. It was already darting through my mind that perhaps I ought to make him a gift of them.

Wine was poured, and the conversation turned to more general topics. Fairfield said he was not very familiar with Hythe, though he had driven through it on his way to Dover. "I have relatives in Dover," he explained.

He mentioned Lympne Castle and Saltwood Castle, where Becket's assassins met en route to Canterbury. Mrs. Lovatt recommended a few old churches he ought to visit, and when his glass was empty, Lord Fairfield rose to take his leave. I accompanied him to the door.

As we reached it, he paused a moment and asked, "When will you be back at Gracefield, ma'am?"

I was so eager for his visit that I said, "I expect we shall leave tomorrow."

"Then I shall call the day after tomorrow. I look forward to seeing you again." He took my hand, but instead of shaking it, he lifted it to within an inch of his lips for a ritual kiss. "I wish it were to be sooner," he added, smiling flirtatiously. I had never seen such beautiful blue eyes. A warmth invaded my cheeks at his manner.

"Can you recommend a good hotel in Hythe?" he continued. "I may wish to remain a few days." His eyes spoke volumes, none of them having to do with pigeons.

"I hope you will stay with us, Lord Fairfield," I said. It seemed the polite thing to do.

"You are very kind, ma'am. I will be honored." He bowed and left.

I wished I could be alone for a moment to savor my little romance, but already Mrs. Lovatt was calling from the sofa corner. "What had he to say, Heather? It took him a long time to leave."

"He was just inquiring where he could stay in Hythe."

"You ought to have asked him to stay at Gracefield, ninny!" my aunt charged.

I had dreaded telling her, lest she think it too forward. "I did," I replied. We exchanged a meaningful smile. Few words are necessary between ladies, where nabbing an eligible parti is concerned.

Smythe shook his head. "Told you, a bit of a dasher. I'll keep an eye on him for you."

"This helps solve the question of Snoad," Mrs. Lovatt said in satisfaction. "Fairfield will take whatever stock is worth anything, and we'll release the rest of them."

"I told him he might come the day after tomorrow, Auntie," I said. "Do you think it too early?"

"Your notices will be in the journals tomorrow," Bunny reminded us. I had forgotten all about them.

"We can have Soames forward any replies to Gracefield," my aunt said. I took it for approval of any early departure. "I am ready to go now. We know what Harold was doing here. Visiting that vulgar hussy. And if he had his fingers into anything else, I don't want to hear any more about it. It is over and done with. We shall leave tomorrow morning. I'm going to retire now. Don't feel you must rush off, Mr. Smythe. You and Heather might want to order some tea later. I cannot take tea before retiring or I am awake all night."

After she was gone, I said, "Perhaps we should remain longer. I feel there is more we could discover here, if we stayed another day."

"She's right. Leads have run out. Our best hope of learning more is to write to Depew and demand a full explanation. About that tea . . ."

I summoned a servant. Fifteen minutes later, there was a tap at the door. The waiter entered, and behind him followed Sir Chauncey Depew.

Until the servant left, the conversation was of a

harmless, social sort. As soon as the door closed behind the waiter, Depew leaned forward eagerly in his chair and said, "Did Fairfield visit you a short while ago, Miss Hume?"

"Yes. How did you know?"

"I've been watching him."

"From where?" Smythe asked. "Spent the afternoon looking for you. Wasn't registered at any of the hotels."

"I am at the Norfolk. I use the name Mr. Martin when I am working on secret matters."

"I knew it!" Smythe exclaimed. "They *are* the prince's buttons."

Depew glanced at his jacket and gave a tsk of dismay. "You are quick to have recognized them, Mr. Smythe. I should not have worn this jacket, but I spilt wine on the only other one I had with me. It is true, I am with the Horse Guards."

"Why was you following Fairfield?" Smythe asked. I listened with my heart in my throat. If Fairfield was an enemy agent, I felt the world had ceased to make sense.

"He is under surveillance," Depew answered cryptically. "I'm not accusing the man of anything, mind. I am just watching him."

"What had he to do with my father's death?" I asked.

"Perhaps nothing. That is precisely what I am trying to discover. I only know that he was here, at this hotel in Brighton, the evening your father was killed. He is usually short of funds, and might have decided to earn some blunt by giving the French a hand."

"There must have been dozens of people here," I

pointed out. "Fairfield follows the pigeon races. That would explain his presence."

"Do they race pigeons from Brighton?" Depew asked, frowning. Neither Smythe nor I actually knew this for a fact, so we said nothing. "Those dozens of others did not return later and ask specifically for this suite," Depew continued.

"You think he was looking for something?" I asked.

"It is a possibility."

"Why was Papa's body spirited off to London? I know he had something to do with spying, so you need not hesitate to tell me on that account."

"So you have figured that out," he said with a worried look. "You are too clever by half! It is true, your father was handling a job for us."

"I see." Though my words were calm, I was delighted and vastly relieved to hear this piece of news.

"No need to go into details. I daresay you have an inkling as to what he was about. As he was a member of the pigeon fanciers' club and went regularly to London on that business, we decided it would cause less curiosity if he simply let the family believe he was visiting London, but came to Brighton instead."

"Would it not have been more convenient for him to work with you in London?" I asked.

"More convenient, but less private. The place is swarming with spies. Your father's—er—lady friend made a good excuse for his visits here."

"Who was it paid for his room?" Smythe asked.

"That was all arranged by London. Our higher class of assistants do not usually accept financial remuneration, but as they are working for us, we treat them a little lavishly."

"I am so glad he was a good spy," I said, inadvertently revealing my fears. "I do not feel so badly about his death, knowing he died in the service of his country."

Depew looked at me as if I were mad. "You cannot have thought Harold Hume was working for the enemy! Good God, he was up for a knighthood! The only delay was in trying to find a suitable pretext for it. We thought perhaps that pigeon strain he bred might provide the excuse, but Lord Castlereagh feared it was a trifle thin. We do not wish to attract any undue attention to him at this time."

"Papa a knight!"

"Perhaps even a baronet," Depew said, nodding wisely. "After the war, of course, when his courage and wisdom could be revealed."

"Could it be done posthumously?" I asked eagerly.

Depew thought about it for a moment. "I'll mention it to Castlereagh. He is the one who traffics in that sort of thing."

"The thing that puzzles me," Smythe said, "where was Mr. Hume done in? Didn't see no blood in the room. Seems no one heard the shot. Demmed odd. Soames told us the hotel's version. A bag of moonshine, I expect."

"It happened here, in this room," Depew said. "We changed the carpet, and put about that the shot was a water jug falling."

"Soames, the clerk here, says you wasn't around, Sir Chauncey," Bunny said, wearing a clever face.

"Naturally a man at my level must never reveal his identity. My men handled the details—not very satisfactorily, I might add. Sending Mr. Hume's clothing home! What a debacle! But that is the way. Impossible to find competent help."

Bunny looked interested. "Glad to give you a hand, Sir Chauncey. Any time."

There was still one major point that I wished to ascertain. "Who killed my father?" I asked.

Depew just shook his head in frustration. "I cannot put a name on him, Miss Hume. There are dozens of spies in Brighton. The French tumbled to it somehow that we were using your father's birds to carry messages. We have a postal system set up with relay points between here and Spain and Portugal. It's faster than sending a man by boat. The foreign birds are shipped to England, and our birds shipped abroad, to bring home news. When urgent word must be sent either way, we use the pigeons. Your father was bringing me a message the day he was killed. I never received it."

"So that's what you're looking for," Bunny exclaimed. "Told you they was looking for something, Heather."

"Did my father have the message on him? As the birds were stolen, too, I wondered if he left the message on the bird."

"Oh no, he carried it on his person. We searched him as soon as we found the body. We searched his room. We had his luggage and carriage taken to London. Our experts went over them with a fine-tooth comb. Nothing. Of course, the French wouldn't know where he carried the message. The birds were the only thing they could readily get their hands on. As they stole the bird cage, I have some hope they did not recover the message from the body before we arrived. In the excitement, we did not think of the bird cage for over an hour. By then, it was gone. But I cannot think your father left the message in an untended cage in the stable."

"The Frenchies got it off his body then," Smythe said. "Pity. Took the bird cage to fool you."

"It looks that way," Depew agreed, "unless Mr. Hume had concealed it in the room. I've searched a dozen times. Hope springs eternal. . . ."

"We looked, too. Course, we didn't know what we was looking for," Bunny said. "I found this." He drew out the feather.

Depew just glanced at it, then turned to me. "Our room was searched this afternoon while we were out," I told him. "By someone who had my father's key." His eyes lit up like a lantern. "Do you think—Fairfield?"

"I was watching him myself. He could have used one of his men, I suppose." He immediately switched to another topic. "One thing that bothers me, Miss Hume, is this Snoad fellow you mention. We did not realize your father had an assistant."

"Yes, Snoad is aware of everything that goes on in the roost. He practically lives there. I find it hard to believe Papa was sending and receiving messages without Snoad's being aware of it."

Depew narrowed his eyes in concentration. "That could explain it—how the Frenchies discovered your father was working with us. Snoad could be the leak. What do you know of him?"

"He used to work for the Duchess of Prescott, with her pigeons," I said. "Do you think he was helping the French?"

"I never like to accuse a man without proof, but on the other hand, I must examine all possibilities.

There must be some reason the duchess turned him off."

"He said it was lung trouble. The doctor recommended sea air. You could write to the duchess."

"I shall. Snoad must be vetted. I'll get on to it at once."

"As you are also keeping an eye on Lord Fairfield," I said, hating to have to say it, "I must tell you, Fairfield is going to Hythe to speak to Snoad the day after tomorrow."

Depew's brows drew together, giving him somewhat the air of an owl. "I see! It is beginning to look black. They must be working together. I must go to Hythe, too," he said.

"To Gracefield?" Bunny asked.

"No, I must play a slier game than that, in case they know me by sight. I'll put up at the inn, but we must keep in close contact. I would prefer that they not know I am in the vicinity. I need eyes and ears working for me at Gracefield. It goes against the grain to enlist civilians, but would it be possible for you to keep me informed, Miss Hume? You could send word to Mr. Martin at the inn if anything unusual occurs. If a pigeon comes in with a message, or—"

"How would I know? Pigeons are coming and going all day. Snoad trains them, you see. They have to be exercized to keep in shape."

"It is a thorny problem," Depew said, shaking his head. "What we have to watch is what they do with any messages that are received. That means keeping a watch on Snoad and Fairfield. I'll have men posted about to follow them if they leave. It would help if you could loiter about the loft as much as possible. Just keep your eyes and ears open. You might happen to be there when a message comes in."

"How is it carried? How would I recognize it?"

"It would be in a specially designed capsule, attached to the bird's leg, most probably. Sometimes it is on the back. Send word to me at once if that occurs. And have a snoop around both their rooms, if you would be so kind."

"Oh dear!" I said. The prospect of snooping through a guest's room, especially a guest like Fairfield, was horrid.

"Think of your father, Miss Hume," he said, and skewered me with a commanding look. "Think of England," he added. The insignificant Depew took on a sort of noble air when he spoke of England in that way.

"Of course," I said.

"Me, too!" Bunny threw in. "I'm good at loitering."

"I shall need all the help I can get," Depew said, smiling his approval.

"What are we looking for?" I asked.

"Anything suspicious—a message, perhaps written in French or Spanish. A little black book. And do you think, ma'am—we might keep it from your aunt? The fewer who know of it, the better. Naturally the entire project is not to be breathed to a soul. Elderly ladies are inclined to chatter. One word in the wrong direction could cost hundreds of lives."

Auntie was not a gossip, but I agreed without question. I felt honored to be involved in such weighty matters. The fate of England might rest, to some degree, on my wits. I had one further point to raise.

"The thing is, Sir Chauncey, my aunt had decided to turn Snoad off almost immediately. We planned to get rid of the pigeons, you see."

"You must talk her out of it! I want Snoad where I can watch him. If he leaves, God only knows where he will go, or what harm he will do. You must not reveal to him that he is under the slightest suspicion. Behave in a perfectly normal way."

"I never had much to do with him," I said.

"No need to change that. You are the owner of Gracefield. He cannot object if you decide to take an interest in your own birds, and spend some time at the loft without making a bosom bow of him."

Truth to tell, it was not his objections I was worried about, but his turning amorous on me if I suddenly began frequenting the loft. There was a certain physical attraction between us, and the projected change in my behavior might mislead him.

"I'll be there if he tries to cut up rusty," Bunny said.

"Yes, you must spend a good deal of time at Gracefield," I said. "Though how I am to explain all these changes to my aunt if she is not to know the whole . . ."

Depew frowned in confusion. "Are you not the mistress of Gracefield, now that your father is dead, Miss Hume? Surely it is for you to make the rules, and your aunt to do as you say, or leave."

"Ye-e-e-s," I said uncertainly. "But Aunt Lovatt is like a second mother to me. I could not offend her."

"It won't be for long," Depew said. "I'll have this little bundle tied up in a day or two, and then you can explain everything to your aunt. Considering the importance of the matter, I do not see what else we can do."

"You're right, of course. And after all this is over, Sir Chauncey, if you would like to appoint a new man to handle the roost, I would be perfectly agreeable for the government to continue using Gracefield as a link in the relay system to our troops in Spain and Portugal."

"Excellent! Excellent," he said, and patted my hand.

He left, with smiles all around. When he was gone, Bunny and I just looked at each other, unable to grasp the enormity of what we had tumbled into.

"We're spies!" Bunny squealed, and threw a cushion into the air in excitement.

"Hush! Auntie will hear you."

"Remember to keep mum," he cautioned. "Whatever you say to your aunt, say nothing."

Never did anyone look less like a spy than Bunny Smythe, unless it might be Miss Hume.

Chapter Seven

My aunt had dozed off by the time I went into the bedroom. The box of sleeping powders on her bedside table told me that my great news, the part of it I could tell her, must wait till morning. As I lay in bed, the peaceful sound of her deep breaths was a counterpoint to the beating of my heart. I was so thrilled with excitement that I forgot the cause of it at first—Papa's death. But a hero's death was different from a meaningless or even shameful shot in the back. I could accept it. If death should likewise come to me in the course of action, I should not feel my life had been in vain. It was a long time before I slept.

I told my aunt the news as soon as she awoke the next morning. "Did I hear Depew's voice, just before I dropped off to sleep?" she asked, drawing back the counterpane.

"Yes, he called. Auntie, you may stop worrying. Papa worked for Sir Chauncey."

Her face drained of color, then turned bright pink

with joy. "Thank God! It's been preying on my mind so. I had to take a powder last night, for I knew I would not shut an eye. My head was aching in three places." This was a headache of major proportions. Auntie's headaches are usually limited to her two temples. Only at times of deep distress does an ache also invade her inner skull. She eagerly demanded details, and while we dressed, I told her all I could remember.

She listened closely, then said, "Harold led us around like a pair of blind ewes, Heather. And to think how often he complimented me that I could see through a double hedge when it came to sly dealings."

I felt a little tremor at my ability to mislead her, but she rattled on. "I think he might have trusted us. I was right about Snoad. We'll give that jackanapes his walking papers the minute we reach home. I never could understand his willingness to settle in a one-eyed little place like Gracefield, when he was used to living in a castle."

Depew wished Snoad to remain. Already my difficulties were beginning, but I would take them one step at a time. "You forget, Lord Fairfield wishes to speak to him. He is not coming until tomorrow. We must let Snoad remain a few days, until we see the flock safely disposed. Lord Fairfield made quite a point of their value."

"Quite right. You'll want to warn Fairfield to be wary of Snoad."

"Good gracious, that is not necessary. What has Fairfield to do with spying? Let us make the visit as pleasant as possible, and not disturb him with thoughts of enemy agents in the house." My beautiful Lord Fairfield—it caused a wrench to have to put him under suspicion. But perhaps he was innocent. Depew had not said for certain that he was guilty.

"It would be a pity to show Lord Fairfield a bad visit," she said. "We'll have to keep an eye on the loft, though. A message might come in from Wellington while Snoad is there alone. That could be fatal to the war."

I had not expected this unwitting assistance from Mrs. Lovatt, but talked up her idea of spending time in the loft as an absolute necessity. "Bunny will help us," I said. "And we could have Snoad followed if he leaves. In case he is taking a message to someone, you know."

"Use your wits, Heather," she said curtly. "He would not *take* it. He would send it by one of the pigeons."

"Oh! I never thought of that!" Nor had Depew. I had inexperience for an excuse, and wondered that Depew was unaware of that possibility. I must warn him of this new problem.

When we were about to go downstairs, I claimed a ladder in my stocking, and told her to go ahead without me. I hastily scribbled a note to Mr. Martin at the Norfolk Inn, and sent it off with a servant before entering the parlor. I tried to make him aware that Snoad must be watched every instant, and suggested that he assign an agent to the loft on a full-time basis. I would convince Snoad that I had hired the man to assist him. Snoad would not like it, but I was fully prepared to remind him who owned the loft, and paid his salary.

Bunny and my aunt had their heads together, deep in conversation, when I joined them. Aunt Lovatt looked up and said, "Mr. Smythe has agreed to spend a few days at Gracefield, Heather. We think it for the best."

"What will you tell your family?" I asked him, not to discourage the scheme, but to lend an air of surprise to the idea.

"Never fear I mean to tell 'em the truth. Wouldn't trust my sisters with a ten-foot pole. Tell 'em I'm thinking of buying the pigeons. They'll cut up stiff. Can't be helped. Mama hates those birds. Never could understand how your mama could stand them, dirtying up the house. I'll tell her I'm leaving them at Gracefield. That should turn the trick."

It sounded perfectly absurd. Bunny had never shown the least interest in the pigeons, but as I needed his assistance, I kept my thoughts to myself. "Three gentlemen in the house!" I said, smiling at the unusualness of the occurrence.

"Three?" my aunt asked. "Why, who else is coming?"

"Lord Fairfield—and Snoad is already there."

"I hope you are not calling that scoundrel a gentleman!" she scoffed.

"Three men, is all I meant," I said, and immediately began pouring coffee.

We packed our belongings and left for Hythe as soon as breakfast was finished. Soames agreed to forward any messages we might receive in reply to our advertisement. We made only one detour to the Pavilion Parade, for it is impossible to pry Auntie loose from Brighton without a trip to the prince's shrine. There it sat, glowing like an Oriental palace, and looking as weird and wonderful as ever, with its onion domes and minarets. We always hoped for a view of the prince, and on that day, our wish was finally gratified.

He was being hoisted onto his mount as we drove past. He slid off, making a most undignified sight. Auntie averted her eyes. "You'd wonder if the earth was still round after that blow," Bunny said, chuckling into his collar.

We decided that the elegant female in the plumed bonnet accompanying him was the Countess de Lieven, and that seemed, in some inexplicable manner, to negate the shame of the prince's tumble. Except for that comic interlude, our trip home was uneventful, unless one can call lunch at Hastings an event. We reached Gracefield around four.

I have mentioned the roost, née widow's walk, of Gracefield. Other than that, I have not given you any idea of the house's architecture. It sits at the top of a cliff, overlooking the sea. The cliff is not very high; it permits clambering down to the shore, which I often do. Gracefield is an ancient old stone heap, which reaches high into the sky, gradually diminishing in floor space as it rises, and terminating in a point, crowned with a weathercock. On the top floor, where Snoad rules, it has only two chambers.

The house always reminds me of a wicked witch's castle when I see it from afar. It is liberally endowed with bartizans, finials, and other accoutrements of romance. The reason I call it a wicked witch's castle is its gloomy aspect. Any of Mrs. Radcliffe's gothic heroines would feel right at home here. The sky is seldom blue. On a good day it is white, but more usually an ominous gray. The ancient trees in the vicinity are warped and twisted from the ocean's wind and salt spray. On a stormy night the wind lashes furiously, and the sea foams up to the top of the little cliff. Safe inside, I adore the violence of those storms.

One odd feature of the house is that it has two fronts. My ancestor who built it wanted an elegant facade to face the ships at sea. His dame wished to impress her neighbors passing it on the road. We therefore have two fine fronts, both with double doors and knockers, and two lesser aspects and doors on either side. Concerned with matters of security, it occurred to me that four doors were a great many to have to contend with, in the matter of anyone leaving—or entering, for that matter. Depew had not thought of that either! We might have unwanted French visitors. I began to see that Depew was not the wizard I had been taking him for. He would want watching.

"Now for a nice cup of tea," Aunt Lovatt said as we dismounted at the front door—the north front door facing the road. "Will you join us, Mr. Smythe?"

She need not have asked. There was no likelihood of Bunny leaving when tea was in the offing. We were met in the hallway by Mrs. Gibbons, a white-haired grenadier of a woman who is the nominal housekeeper, although Mrs. Lovatt makes all the important decisions.

"Thank God you're home!" Mrs. Gibbons said. I had the feeling she was about to fall to her knees in gratitude to the divinity. Her face was as long as the long-case clock in the saloon, and she spoke with such force that we were all thrown into alarm.

"What on earth has happened?" Mrs. Lovatt demanded.

"Burglars!" she declared. "Someone busted in

last night and ransacked Mr. Hume's office. Every book in the place was tossed onto the floor. Snoad has given us a hand tidying it up, as he knows where everything goes. He just went back up to the roost."

Without further talk, we all four headed to the office, where Snoad had performed his job so thoroughly that no one would ever know it had been disarranged.

"How did the man get in?" I asked.

"The door on the east side was jimmied open. Thumm has fixed it up as best he could." Thumm, while nominally our butler, is a clever hand at general work as well.

"Did anyone catch a sight of the man?" I asked.

"We had no idea he'd been here till I sent Mary into the office to dust this morning, and she saw the mess. I called the constable from Hythe, miss. He's making inquiries."

"That's fine, Mrs. Gibbons. I'll just have a look around and see if I notice anything missing."

"Snoad says there's nothing taken. An odd thing entirely. The man could have carried away the silverware, for the dining room's just down the hall, but he didn't take a thing. I've checked it all out. Not so much as a teaspoon is gone, thank the Lord."

Of course, it was not teaspoons he was after, but information. It was not likely the message Papa had been carrying was here. Perhaps he was after the schedule of messages expected, or some notes regarding messages to be sent.

Mrs. Lovatt rushed out with Mrs. Gibbons to examine the east door. Bunny remained behind with me. It was my first chance for a private word with him, and I told him about the note I had written to

Depew, and my fear for the excess of doors at Gracefield.

"We can bar the doors at night," he said. "Ram a chair under the knob. I'll sleep downstairs. I'll hear if anyone jiggles them aside and gets in."

"Do you have a gun, Bunny?"

"I have my shooting guns at home."

"Papa has a pistol in the bottom drawer of his desk. I'll get it for you." I went to the desk and drew open the drawer. The gun was gone. I don't know whether it was fear or anger that caused the rush of blood to my head. I must stay calm. Perhaps Mrs. Gibbons had taken the gun after the break-in.

"It's gone," I told Bunny, and rushed off after Mrs. Gibbons to inquire for the pistol.

"What pistol?" she asked, horrified. "I had no idea your father kept a pistol in his office. Whatever did he do that for?"

She was still jabbering when I returned to the study, and Bunny. "I think we know now what the break-in was all about," I said.

"How would the fellow who got in know the gun was there?"

"He wouldn't, but Snoad knew this office like the back of his hand."

"Then he could have just lifted it and kept mum."

"He knew I spent time here. He needed some explanation if I should discover the pistol was missing. So he made a stage play of someone having broken in, and just took the gun himself." I kept my main concern to myself. What did Snoad want with a gun, if he was not planning to shoot someone? I remembered that hole in Papa's jacket, and the blood on his shirt.

Bunny listened, nodding his agreement. "Believe

I'll just nip down to the inn and leave off a note for Mr. Martin."

"He didn't tell us what inn he was going to." More amateurishness on Depew's part.

"White Hart," Bunny said with an air of certainty.

"Did he tell you so?"

"Nope. Everyone stays at the White Hart."

With the Swan and the Red Lion and any number of decent hostelries doing a brisk business, I could not be so sure Depew would choose the White Hart, but Bunny had a nice knowledge of social customs. That, if nothing else, he had got from his one term at Cambridge.

"If I get a wiggle on, I can be back for tea. Good thing I left my mount here," he said, and left.

I sank onto the chair behind Papa's desk to consider what I should do. My orders were to keep an eye on the loft, and much as I dreaded facing Snoad, the robbery gave me an excellent excuse for going up there. I was just taking myself by the scruff of the neck to do it when there was a tap at the open door. Looking up, I saw Snoad standing in the doorway.

He had put on a cravat and jacket to come belowstairs. In the dimness of the doorway, he might be mistaken for a gentleman. In any light, there was no ignoring his physical beauty. Yet it was a foreign sort of beauty, dark of hair and flashing of eye, like the more interesting sort of Frenchman.

When he had caught my attention, he stepped in. "You heard the news?" he asked. I sensed the excitement in him. He was worried lest I suspect him.

I quickly scanned what tack I should take, and remembered Depew's advice. Behave as if you suspect nothing. "Yes indeed, Mrs. Gibbons has told us. Such an odd robbery, with nothing taken."

"Robbery?" he asked in surprise. "I don't think it was a simple robbery."

"Oh really? What do you think, Snoad?" I asked, adopting a wide-eyed air of simplicity.

He bit his lip, as if regretting his rash words. "I daresay you're right," he said. "But Mrs. Gibbons said none of the silver was gone. The only thing missing is your father's gun, Miss Hume."

Now, why the devil had he told me? Pointing it out might, perhaps, direct suspicion away from himself if it was discovered later. "Really!" I said, feigning fright. "Where did Papa keep it?"

"In this drawer," he said, moving behind the desk to slide open the bottom drawer. His head was bent down, just inches below me. I noticed how rich and full his hair grew, and how crow black it was, with tints of color in the light from the window. Then he looked up, and I was struck anew with the splendor of his eyes. They were a brownish black shade, like coffee, with lashes a lady might envy.

"I wonder how he knew it was there," I said.

"Most men keep a gun in their offices, I believe."

"I hope he does not plan to return and use it on us."

His lips moved in a soft smile. White teeth gleamed behind his full lips. "A good thing I'm here to protect you, miss," he said, in a gentle voice.

I felt like a mouse under the protection of a wild cat. He rose from the drawer and resumed a businesslike pose, and my heart resumed its normal beat. He spoke on about having tidied up the office, and nothing being stolen, so far as he could tell.

I only half listened. What I was telling myself

was that from an objective point of view, Snoad was no worse than I. He was a Frenchman—surely he was not English—spying for France. I was an English lady, spying for England. We were equals in that respect. I thought, too, that the French would not choose those of low birth for such important work. Perhaps Snoad was wellborn, though not a nobleman, of course. The revolution had pretty well decimated that breed. Those who had escaped to England would be in no hurry to lend Boney a hand. I decided he was a gentleman. I could not despise the man for bravery and patriotism. But I could and did regret that we were on opposite sides in the battle.

Then I remembered that he had been at Branksome Hall for two years, and all my romantic fabrication unraveled in a trice. Snoad was no French gentleman spy. He was an English servant with ambitions to make himself a fortune, and did not care if he had to abet the enemy to do it. Or to connive at my father's death.

"How did it go in Brighton?" he asked.

Before I could reply, Aunt Lovatt came to the door. "The tea is ready, Heather," she said. She bridled up like an angry mare when she saw Snoad. I hoped she would not say something very rude to him. She said nothing. I knew she could not trust herself to speak.

"We'll speak about it later, Snoad," I said, and went out with my aunt.

Chapter Eight

With his own excellent bit of blood under him, and the lure of tea to hasten his trip, Bunny was back before the pot was cold. Nothing could be said about our work in front of my aunt, but as soon as she left, I asked him if he had found Depew.

"Mr. Martin is registered at the White Hart." Bunny was right about which hotel he would choose. "Wasn't in at the moment. Left him a note. Told him I'd be staying here for the nonce."

"Good. I wonder how he'll contact us."

"We ought to select a place to leave notes. The old blasted pine—we could use that."

It would have been my own choice. Lightning had split one of the ancient pines in the park. What remained was a topless trunk with one branch within arm's reach, to provide concealment. The tree could not be seen from the house, but it was an easy dart to reach it. "I'll suggest it to him next time we meet." I told him about my interview with

Snoad, and that I planned to go to the loft to continue it.

"I'll go with you," he offered at once.

"There is something more important you should do, Bunny. Do you have a gun at home?"

"A whole wall full of them. So has your papa, come to that."

"A pistol is what I meant. Something easy to handle and conceal. You should go home and get it. And really, you know, you should visit your mother and tell her you're staying here. There's time to do it before dinner."

"I'd best do it, or I'll never hear the end of it. I need some clean linen besides."

He left, and I went upstairs for my meeting with Snoad, thinking about what story I would tell him. I was to be ignorant of any spy dealings, which meant Papa's murder must be either senseless, or involve Mrs. Mobley and a jealous lover. I could not like to lumber my father with a tasteless posthumous scandal involving that woman, so I opted for an accidental slaying.

I would keep my eyes and ears open while I was with Snoad. Now that I knew him for a villain, I might pick up something I had overlooked before.

The loft was unchanged, so far as I could tell at a glance. Snoad still wore his jacket and cravat, which looked out of place as he was sweeping the floor. He looked up when he heard the door close.

"I was just preparing for your visit," he said, lifting the broom. I thought he was embarrassed to be caught at such a low job. But then, it was one of his regular duties, so there was no reason he should be.

"It looks very tidy."

He set the broom aside and came to meet me. "You were going to tell me how things went in Brighton," he said.

The seating arrangements in the loft were primitive. Two abandoned kitchen chairs and a deal table had been brought up. They were discolored from exposure to the damp, so I avoided them. We walked back and forth along the parapet as we talked.

"It was very curious," I said. "The police were not at all helpful. No one saw the murder."

"Where was the body found? In the hotel, or in some back alley?"

I hesitated a moment, and decided against the hotel. To add a touch of veracity, I chose a specific location. "At the fish market. Perhaps he was going to bring us home some fresh fish."

Snoad listened, tension in every line of his body. "So he was killed in Brighton then."

Now, too late, I wondered if I should have opted for London. "Yes," I said.

"He wasn't buying fish. More likely it was an assignation. He was not planning to return till the next afternoon. He wouldn't buy fish so early in his visit. What time of day was he killed? Evening, I assume."

"Yes, the body was found around dinnertime."

"Did the constable tell you why it was taken to London?"

"No."

"He must have given *some* excuse," Snoad persisted. He was a close questioner!

"They—there was no identification on him. They thought he was a Londoner, just down for a visit, and took his body there."

"But his wallet was returned with his body. He carried his calling cards in it."

"It must have been at the hotel."

"He wouldn't go out without it. If the police knew he was staying at the Royal Crescent, then they would have no trouble discovering who he was. There's something havey cavey about this."

I was becoming annoyed at Snoad's curiosity and spoke sharply. "The constable was not very helpful. The man who actually handled the case was not working yesterday. The other one, the one who attended us, had only the report to go by."

"And you're going to leave it like this?" he demanded angrily. "Your father is murdered, and you stay only half a day, without even speaking to the constable who found him?"

"We put notices in the journals. If anyone saw anything, they will be in touch with us. What do you expect of me? He's dead. Prying into it is not going to bring him back."

"By God, if it were my father who had been shot, I would make more effort than this to find his assassin, and kill him."

"Well, he was *not* your father. He was mine, and if there were any evidence, you may be sure I would follow it up. I would stop at nothing to get revenge on whoever harmed him. That poor, innocent man. Someone ought to pay. I am satisfied, however, that it was a senseless slaying. Some footpad got hold of him and shot him and disappeared into the night without leaving a trace."

"A footpad shot him in the back? Without removing his watch and wallet? I had not thought you were so gullible, or so disinterested in your father."

The ferocity of his attack astonished me. Shock

soon gave way to anger. "You are forgetting your place, Snoad. He was my father. How I handle his death is no concern of yours."

"It ought to be someone's concern. Next you will tell me you plan to set the birds free, or have them shot."

"Certainly not," I replied smugly. "Lord Fairfield will be coming to look them over tomorrow, and take those that he wants for his own collection. He is particularly interested in Caesar and Cleo, for breeding purposes. Where is Caesar?"

An angry spark flared in his black eyes. "I see! So that explains it. It is the dashing Lord Fairfield who has put your father's death out of your mind."

A pigeon, interested in our talk, flew down from a roost and perched on Snoad's shoulder. He brushed it away impatiently. I noticed a small metal ring just above its foot. The sort of ring that a message might be attached to. It registered in the back of my mind, without interrupting the flow of argument.

"You are impertinent, sir! Remember you are here at my pleasure. If you wish to continue in this position, you will behave yourself properly."

Anger warred with necessity. Snoad swallowed his anger, and his pride, and apologized, because he was determined not to be ousted from this loft. "I'm sorry. You are quite right, Miss Hume. I let myself be carried away by my concern for Mr. Hume." His smoldering eyes were a reminder of my lack of concern. I was sorry to give him such a poor opinion of me, and annoyed with myself for caring a groat what he thought.

"I expect Lord Fairfield tomorrow. He will want to see what you are doing here. He is very interested in my father's work. I will expect you to show him what he wishes to see. I'll just have a look around and see that everything is tidy."

This was a mere pretext for snooping. I don't know what I expected to find. If he had stolen the pistol, it was unlikely he had stashed it in a pigeon's nest. Snoad forced himself to civility and accompanied me, to prevent me from finding anything.

The loft had rows of boxes built one on top of the other, rather like a bookcase with compartments. The nesting birds had built extremely insubstantial-looking nests in them with twigs and straw and weeds. Snoad lifted one to show me a clutch of two white eggs. The brooding bird attacked with the angry vigor of a swan, and I leapt away in fright. "She did not like our prying," I said.

"Actually, that was a he. I told you the males incubate by day. They're touchy when they're nesting," Snoad explained.

Other birds had already hatched. I had a fairly gross exhibition of a parent feeding its young. The chick stuck its head right into the parent's mouth, and looked as if it were being swallowed alive and whole. Snoad assured me it was merely taking pigeon's milk from the crop.

As we came to the end of the nests, we discovered a little commotion. A group of birds, about a dozen in all, were strutting around, not in circles, but as if examining each other. They were cooing in a deep, throaty way, more loudly than the pigeons usually do. Some of them were raising their wings, and others were pecking angrily at one another. I would have taken it for a mating ritual, except that so many of the birds were angry, and fighting the advancer off.

"Is this some territorial war?" I asked. "Is the loft overcrowded?" I had seen something similar when we had too many hens in the yard.

Snoad's smirk told me I had asked the wrong question. "I am surprised a farmer's daughter does not recognize the mating ritual of birds," he said.

"It did occur to me, but why are so many of the females rejecting their would-be suitors?"

"Is that so unusual?" he inquired, with a laughing eye. I gave him a glacial stare that brought him back to propriety.

"The fact is, what you are calling females are males," he explained. "Unlike many species, the males have no physical embellishment. The pigeons cannot tell by appearance whether they are dealing with a male or a female. They must go by trial and error, and have to take many a peck before they find a mate. When you see a bird edging shyly away from another's advances, and acting as if she could not care less, then you know that is a female. The males of the species are more forthright. They give the fellow a sharp peck, take a flying leap at him, and he leaves them alone."

I found this talk slightly broad, and turned my gaze seaward.

"Folks have a peculiarly personal reaction to animals' mating," Snoad said pensively. "It is a natural function, like eating or walking. Odd that we should feel embarrassed."

I did not wish to appear a prude, though it was obvious to me that there is a difference between eating and mating. I took an unconcerned glance at the performing birds. One male had found an acquiescent female, and was, I feared, about to have his way with her. I hastily averted my eyes and began to walk away. Snoad remained behind, studying them.

"I think even birds would like privacy at a time like this, Snoad," I said sharply.

"I want to see this."

"Voyeur!"

"I must check to see who Queenie is mating with" was his excuse. "These are valuable birds. I think—yes, by God, she's chosen Alphonse. Now, that surprises me. I was sure the Captain had the inner track. He's been wooing her all week."

"If they mate for life, you will soon know which she has chosen."

"I must also record the date and time of mating. Your father kept strict, accurate records. I plan to continue his method. Ah, look at the poor Captain, dragging his tail behind him. Cut to the quick by Queenie's fickleness."

I just glanced at the birds, making sure to avoid the mating pair.

"The Captain was the better man—er, bird." He finally pulled himself away from the spectacle and joined me. "There is no accounting for ladies' taste. When did you say Lord Fairfield is coming?"

I gave him a sharp look, wondering if the sudden mention of Fairfield was intentional. His eyes were brimming with laughter.

"Tomorrow," I said, refusing to recognize any ulterior meaning in the question. "Everything seems in order here. You'll remember to give me the bill for the feed you mentioned the other day."

"It was evening when we first ... became friends," he said, just hesitating over the last words.

I gave him another icy look. "I'll take it to your office this evening, Miss Hume."

"I shan't be in my office this evening, but you may leave it there."

"Surely you could arrange to be there for a few minutes. Say, about eight-thirty?" He peered down at me with a conning look.

"I have company this evening."

"I thought Fairfield was coming tomorrow."

"Lord Fairfield is coming tomorrow. Mr. Smythe is spending a few days with us."

"Is there a special reason?" he asked.

It was none of his business, but I did not wish to arouse his curiosity and said, "After the break-in, my aunt feels we require a man about the house. Thumm is getting on, you know."

"But you have a younger man, Miss Hume. I would be happy to sleep downstairs—if it would make you feel safer." He kept his lips steady during this studied piece of impertinence.

"That is very kind, but unnecessary. Good day, Snoad."

He gave his forelock a playful tug and bobbed his head. "I was honored by your visit, your ladyship. I hope you will come again." Then his grin dwindled to a nice smile, and he added, "Soon—and often."

"I shouldn't think that will be necessary," I said grandly, and regretted it as soon as I had strode away. Because my duty *would* bring me back soon, and often. It was not an unpleasant duty either. Snoad was an accomplished flirt. I decided that a lady might enjoy a small flirtation with her servant without wounding her dignity.

While I was in my room, checking that my unpacking had been executed to my satisfaction, I reviewed that visit with Snoad. "The dashing Lord Fairfield," he had said. How did Snoad know what Fairfield was like?

Was Depew correct in his suspicions of Lord Fairfield? Were he and Snoad working together? I remembered that bird with the ring around its ankle, too, but there had been no message attached to it. Like a ninny, I never gave another thought to one question I had asked, and failed to get answered. Caesar had not been in his tree, nor had he been in Cleo's nest. He had not been in the loft the other day either. But I did not think of that at all. I had been too diverted by Snoad's expert flirtation.

Chapter Nine

Nothing of great interest happened during the remainder of the day and evening. Bunny returned with his pistol. We had the servants set a truckle bed up for him in Papa's office, and hid the pistol under the pillow for easy access, if it should prove necessary. Bunny went up to keep an eye on Snoad and returned to inform me Snoad was awake on all suits. "Asked a hundred questions, but I fooled him. Didn't answer anything to the point."

I did not return to the loft again, nor did I visit Papa's office at eight-thirty. Now that Bunny and I were spies, we took a keener interest in the war, and studied the journals to learn in detail how matters were progressing abroad. We learned that since Napoleon's defeat in Moscow the year before, he had had to withdraw troops home from the Peninsula. It seemed the Spanish guerrillas were keeping four French divisions busy in Biscay and Navarre. Wellington had marched from Portugal. The French were falling back to the Ebro.

There was a suggestion that Napoleon must send more forces to Spain. Bunny thought this was a clue that the English would attack before they could arrive. We both thought that my father's birds were carrying messages on this weighty matter back and forth along the postal relay route.

"The duke will run those Frenchies right back over the Pyrenees," Bunny said, eyes gleaming. "And we'll help him, by jingo." I gave him a warning glare.

"How will you do that, Mr. Smythe?" my aunt asked indulgently, and fortunately did not wait for a reply. "What has caused this sudden interest in the war?"

I answered swiftly, before Bunny revealed more than he ought. "Why, because of Papa's work, of course," I said. It is always best to stick to the truth when possible.

"That is what I thought." She nodded, satisfied. "It all seems more relevant, somehow, when a loved one is involved."

Later Bunny announced that he was going up to the loft to blow a cloud with Snoad. He narrowed his eyes at me in a meaningful way, but I didn't know what he meant. When he returned, he managed a moment's privacy to tell me his real motive had been to search Snoad's rooms. "Keeps his rooms locked. Looks pretty suspicious, eh? Where could we find a key?"

We searched Papa's office, but without luck. "The time to do it is when Snoad is out," I decided. "He will have to take the birds out to continue their training sooner or later." He was not likely to do it at this hour of the night, however.

We retired early, and rose early the next morning to prepare for Lord Fairfield's visit. The whole house was in confusion, with servants applying beeswax and turpentine to the furnishings, and sprinkling tea leaves over the carpets to keep down the dust when they swept them. The kitchen, I knew, would be in an uproar. There was talk of a suckling pig, and the tantalizing aroma of cakes and pastries filled the house.

My own special contribution was to see to the preparation of the Gold Suite for our guest. This is the best guest suite, with a view of the ocean in front, and of the park on the east. I oversaw the servants' work, and arranged a bouquet of flowers from the conservatory. Bunny selected a bottle of Papa's best sherry from the cellar, and another of claret, "in case he's a red wine man."

Bunny made another trip into Hythe, and finally spoke with Depew. "What did he say about the note I left him in Brighton? I am worried that Snoad might be sending messages out by the pigeons," I said when he returned.

"He hadn't received your note."

"I sent it to his hotel in Brighton. It must have been intercepted by the French. I daresay every step Depew takes is watched."

"Very likely. And us, too, for all we know." We exchanged an important look, and peered around for listeners.

"I fear he is quite ignorant of how the pigeon relay operates, Bunny. Snoad could be sending messages off to France while we sit on our thumbs. I must arrange a visit with Depew."

"Said he'd be in touch. Told him about the blasted pine in the park."

We made a dash out to it, but there was no message. In case I did not see Depew when he came, I wrote down how the pigeons operated, and stuck the letter in the pine. Bunny came with me.

"Depew says he's pretty well convinced Fairfield is in on it," he said. "Dipped. Doing it for money. Says to be sure you don't let out that he's here; Depew, I mean. Er, Martin. We're only to refer to him as Mr. Martin, in case they're eavesdropping."

"It's very exciting, is it not?" I asked, looking around the park to see if I could spot any of our cohorts, as Depew had said he would post men. They were so proficient that I could not spot them, but it felt good, knowing they were there. The glory of it filled me with joy. It was an exultant feeling, like being in love. My whole body seemed more alive, almost glowing.

"Demmed exciting." Bunny smiled. I knew by the gleam in his eyes that he felt the same way. "Heroes, in a way."

"Perhaps you will be given a baronetcy when it is over, Bunny. Sir Horatio Smythe."

"They'll have to make you a baroness—er, baronetess."

"Perhaps a dame," I mused. "Dame Heather Hume has a nice ring, has it not?"

"Dandy. Would you get the sword over the shoulder, like a knight?"

"I don't know. I shouldn't think they tap very hard."

"We might get invited to the Royal Pavilion. Aunt Lovatt would like that."

We were interrupted by the clatter of wheels from the road. Glancing down, we espied an elegant black chaise with a lozenge on the door, followed by a curricle, trailing a mount.

"Fairfield," Bunny said. "Why the devil has he brought so many rigs and prads? Looks as if he plans to stay a month. Look at all the servants you'll have to feed! Two drivers; there'll be a valet in that chaise with him for certain. Fairfield's a famous dandy. Hard to believe he's a spy. Don't usually care for anything but his nags and jackets. A dandy bit o' blood," he added, gazing at the bay mare that trotted smartly along behind the curricle, breathing dust. "I wouldn't mind throwing a leg over her."

"We'd best go in to greet him."

We returned, entered by the side door, and ran immediately to the north front door, which we call the road door. Thumm had thrown the portals wide, giving us a view of Fairfield's carriage, drawing to a stop with a jingle of harnesses. A liveried footman hopped out to open the carriage door. I mentally added another servant to the list of mouths to be fed. Another head in the carriage proved to be his valet.

As Lord Fairfield stood, gazing at the house through his quizzing glass, all the bother seemed worthwhile. He had removed his curled beaver. His golden head glinted in the pale sunlight that penetrated the white cloud covering. His broad shoulders, his elegant biscuit pantaloons and Hessians, were all in the latest jet of fashion.

I noticed Bunny looking down at his own country breeches and top boots with dissatisfaction. While we gazed, the quizzing glass was lowered and Fairfield lunged forward, throwing some comment over his shoulder to his footman in a splendidly cavalier fashion.

Aunt Lovatt rushed up behind me, all out of

breath. "He's here!" she exclaimed. "Oh my! What a lot of carriages and servants." There was no dismay in her accents. She was highly impressed at this lavish display.

When Fairfield discovered the welcoming committee hovering inside the door, he gave one of his dazzling smiles. The golden head inclined, and he said, "Miss Hume."

I curtsied. "We are very happy to welcome you to Gracefield, milord."

He stepped in. "Not nearly so happy as I am to be here, ma'am. A very interesting house. I look forward to exploring it."

Aunt Lovatt and Bunny came forward to curtsy and shake hands respectively. After a general commotion of greetings, we invited our guest into the saloon for tea. Thumm would handle the servants and the disposition of the trunks. And hopefully warn our groom to get in a good supply of hay and oats for all those horses.

I was hard-pressed to remember it was possibly a spy I was entertaining with Cook's mutton and tea cakes. It seemed impossible that Fairfield should be involved in anything underhanded. There was a guileless air about the man, and an innocence in his noble blue eyes.

"Such an interesting house," he said more than once. "Quite like a fairy castle. Does it have a ghost?"

"No, not even a secret passage," I confessed.

"It must surely have an interesting history at least. So conveniently located for smuggling brandy. How I wish one of Papa's houses was on the sea. All our places are landlocked. The castle in Hampshire, the hunting lodge in the Cottswolds, and the estate my uncle Eustace left us in Scotland are all boring old heaps. Of course, the London house is no more than a free hotel for relatives."

"Pity," Bunny said, without the least shred of sarcasm.

"Mind you, we have an oubliette at the castle," Fairfield added, with all the enthusiasm of a boy. "I scratched a message on the wall to fool Algernon. That's my younger brother. He is a captain in the Guards," he added, proud of this accomplishment. Surely a lord with a brother in the army would not be a spy! Snoad must be duping him, as he had duped Papa.

"What message?" Bunny asked.

"I wrote, 'Good-bye, cruel world. I am innocent of the crimes ascribed to me by the wicked Marquess of Albemarle.' That is my papa's title. Well, one of them. The one he uses."

"What crime?" Bunny asked.

Fairfield blinked rather stupidly. "There was no crime. It was a joke," he explained.

Bunny said, "Oh." Then he laughed dutifully.

Aunt Lovatt said, "I am sorry we will not be able to offer you much in the way of entertainment, milord, but as you know, we are in mourning."

"I would not be here if you weren't." He frowned at this rather ambiguous speech and said, "What I mean is, the pigeons would not be for sale if Mr. Hume were still alive." It was a hard remark to reply to. After a short pause, Fairfield continued with a bow in my direction. "The pigeons will be entertainment enough for me."

His quizzing smile seemed almost to include me amongst the entertaining pigeons. There was an air of admiration in it.

As we had finished tea, I said, "Would you like to go up and see them now, Lord Fairfield?"

"Indeed I would. I am most eager to go." In his eagerness, he leapt to his feet. I rose to accompany him. "You need not bother to show me the way, Miss Hume. A servant . . ." He looked around, but our servants were not so plentiful that we kept them on hand to pass us a piece of cake, or fill a teacup.

"This way," I said, and he followed me.

"Do you want me to go with you?" Bunny asked.

I had assumed he would, yet could not like to ask for his escort. That was as good as an announcement that I did not trust Fairfield.

"I shall see that Miss Hume is safe on the staircase," Lord Fairfield said, and took my elbow to lead me off toward the dining room.

"It is this way," I said, steering him right.

"I was always interested in these old historical homes," he said as we climbed. This compliment was wearing a trifle thin, but I smiled my pleasure and kept climbing.

"It's a lot of stairs, is it not?" he asked as we reached the third floor.

"It is not much farther, milord."

His conversation gave way to panting. I pointed out a few of the house's highlights. "Charles Fox stayed in that room," I said.

"On the servants' floor!" he exclaimed.

"There was a boxing match in the neighborhood. Every room was filled when he arrived unexpectedly. He wanted no more than two chairs and a bolster by the fireplace."

"Who was boxing?" he asked. That was his only interest in the illustrious Fox. Lord Fairfield, I feared, was not one of those gentlemen who im-

115

proved on longer acquaintance. His appearance and manners were good, so that he made a fine first impression, but already he was beginning to seem shallow.

"I believe one of them was called the Tin Man."

"By Jove! Wouldn't I like to have seen that."

We finally reached the loft. Fairfield was puffing like a winded jade, which surprised me. I had thought a Corinthian would be in better shape. Snoad was sitting on one of the mildewed chairs reading a book when we entered. He rose and hastened forward. His employer, myself, did not receive such condescension.

"Lord Fairfield, this is—"

Snoad stuck out his hand and gave Fairfield's a wrench. "Snoad. I tend the pigeons."

"This is Lord Fairfield," I said with a heavy frown. I disliked his eagerness to rub shoulders with the nobility.

"Don't I know you?" Fairfield said, examining Snoad with keen interest.

"I believe we met at Branksome Hall three years ago, your lordship. Kind of you to remember."

"Of course! Branksome Hall. The duke had a hurdle race."

"And you won. Fine riding, your lordship. I helped to set up the hurdles, and gave a hand with the horses." The day obviously stood out more sharply in Snoad's memory than in Fairfield's. Fairfield wrinkled his brow, but did not appear to remember the details. "You were driving Beelzebub, an Arab gelding," Snoad prodded him.

"I would like you to give me a hand showing Lord Fairfield the pigeons, Snoad," I said, to bring his groveling to a halt.

He bowed to our guest. "It would be a great pleasure, your lordship."

He took Fairfield by the arm and began walking along the row of nests. I lingered behind, because I wanted to see what Snoad had been reading with such avid interest. Imagine my surprise when it turned out to be a book of poems by Lord Byron. I soon espied something more suspicious. There was a piece of paper stuck into the book, and a patent pen on the table beside it. I had to see what he had been writing. I picked up the book, glancing to see that Snoad was not watching. He turned and leveled a menacing look at me. I set the book down.

It was as clear as could be that he was writing up some spy message. Fortunately, Fairfield distracted Snoad with a question, and I was able to slide the piece of paper out without disturbing the book. I strolled to the other end of the loft, and with my back to them, read the paper. I had another shock in store for me. It was a poem, a love poem to a lady. It was entitled "Dove."

I read:

> Dove gray her eyes,
> Dove soft her sighs.
> In moonlight or sunlight,
> Love-soft the ties
> That bind me.

> Alone in the cloud
> Too fierce and too proud
> To open my mad heart.
> No love avowed.
> Joy found me.

I stood a moment, staring at it. Was it a coded message? Or was it what it seemed, a love offering to his lady with the gray eyes? Whatever it was, I had to get it back into the book before Snoad realized I had seen it. While the men were busy at one of the nests, I quickly returned and slid the paper back into the book. Then I walked nonchalantly along and joined them.

"Where are the males while the females are hatching the eggs?" Fairfield asked.

"They're about the loft," Snoad replied. I remembered him telling me that it was the males who sat on the eggs during the day. Why did he not tell Fairfield? And even more interesting, why did Fairfield not know it, if he was a breeder as he claimed to be?

A little later, Fairfield expressed some surprise that so many of the nests held two eggs. Two glossy white eggs were the standard. Really, the man was even more ignorant about the whole business than I was.

"All of this is old hat to Miss Hume," Snoad said. "Do not let us keep you, ma'am, if you have other business to attend to."

I had no intention of letting him run me off, and said, "It is Caesar and Cleo that Lord Fairfield is particularly interested in. Where are they? I have not seen them any of the times I have been up here recently."

"Cleo is in the tree, waiting for Caesar to return," he said. I looked, and saw a bird that might have been Cleo sitting in the tree. She was almost all white, with a splash of burgundy on her chest. Her maternal grandmother was a passenger pigeon from America. Pelletier had introduced the strain into his roost for their superior size. The fleshy protuberance at the base of her beak—Papa called it a cere—was also distinctive. It was darker than most, almost black. That she dared to sit in that tree was proof enough that she was indeed Caesar's mate. No other birds dared to touch it. Caesar had a sharp temper.

Yet the other day, he had told me Cleo was nesting. He had said Caesar was with her. "Where is Caesar?" I asked.

"He got bored, and is out for a flight," Snoad replied. "While you are here, ma'am, there is something I would like to discuss with you. Now that your father is not here, I really need a helper. The birds being trained must be taken some miles from the loft and released on a regular basis, so they will learn to fly home. I shall need someone in the loft while I take the birds away, or someone to take them while I remain here."

"I'd be happy to do it," Lord Fairfield said.

"But you will only be here a few days, milord," Snoad pointed out.

"If you'll cage the birds, I'll have the groom take them out," I told Snoad. "Just tell him where you wish them to be taken."

"It would be better if you could let me have a footman on a regular basis—one person that I could give some rudimentary training," Snoad persisted.

I didn't like to quibble in front of Fairfield, and agreed, sullenly, to let him have the use of the backhouse boy and a jig for a part of each day. I was thoroughly bored, but Fairfield seemed to have an inexhaustible interest in the pigeons. After the better part of an hour, I spotted Bunny in the park and left the loft.

Bunny was just returning from the direction of the blasted pine. I dashed out to meet him. "A note from Depew—er, Martin," he said excitedly. "He's coming tonight—eleven o'clock, at the tree."

"Excellent! I have dozens of things to tell him. Fairfield is a phony, and Snoad is writing up some cryptic messages."

"Did you get hold of them?"

"I caught a glimpse of one. He is hiding the message in a poem. I tried to memorize it. It was short." We went to Papa's study, and I wrote out what I could remember of the few lines.

"Sounds like a love poem," Bunny said. "Dashed pretty."

"Don't be foolish. It is a message to the French. What can it mean? He mentions moonlight, you see. That could refer to the time of an attack, or a troop movement, or some such thing."

"What do you figure that bit about alone in the cloud means?"

"Fierce and proud sounds like Napoleon."

"Except he is not alone in a cloud. Almost sounds like God."

"We'll let Mr. Martin decipher this," I said, and hid the copy in my pocket.

It was time to dress for dinner. I looked forward to our first formal meal with Lord Fairfield. "Keep him as long as you can over port, after dinner. I'll go up and search his rooms."

"Wish I could go with you."

"Your role is equally important, Bunny. You are the only other gentleman here, so you must delay Fairfield, to make it safe for me to do the job. We are a team."

"By Jove, it makes a fellow feel good to be doing

something real for a change. I just wish we could tell everyone."

"We must not breathe a word!"

"Mum's the word."

On this solemn speech, we parted. I checked the afternoon post. There were no replies to our advertisement in the Brighton journals, nor did I expect any.

Chapter Ten

The feast that Cook provided was excellent. Other than that, dinner with a baron proved very little different from dinner with the vicar, or any provincial neighbor. The gentlemen pretty well monopolized the conversation, as gentlemen in the country generally do. I daresay society matrons know a few tricks to divert the talk from horses, but neither Mrs. Lovatt nor I possessed this desirable skill.

"A dandy-looking bay mare you brought along, Lord Fairfield," Bunny said.

"I got her for an old song off Alvanley. He has a hunter I have my eye on as well."

"I'll tell you where you can get a good hunter, and it won't cost you a limb either. Singer, right in Hythe, has one for sale. Bred and trained in Ireland. A dandy jumper. Straight off her hocks, she can leap Soper's fence. She's a good hacker, too. She knows which side of the road is up."

"Perhaps you can introduce me to Singer."

"Gladly."

"How's the riding hereabouts?"

"Heather enjoys riding," Mrs. Lovatt said, to put me forward.

Fairfield passed along an impatient smile, before turning for Bunny's answer. That was the way the entire two courses and two removes went. I was impatient to leave the gentlemen to their port, and get upstairs to root about Fairfield's rooms.

At the proper time, Auntie and I retired to the drawing room. "What a charming man Lord Fairfield is," Auntie said.

"He is certainly handsome," I allowed.

"And rich! All those houses he will inherit!"

"And an oubliette," I added, with a teasing smile. "Come now, Auntie, you must admit he is no conversationalist."

"Pooh! What has conversation to do with anything? You would be a baroness, and a marchioness one day, lording it over London society. You always wanted a Season."

To escape without suspicion, I said, "In that case, I had best go upstairs and refurbish my toilette."

"Such a pity we are in mourning, and cannot show Lord Fairfield a livelier time. Do you think, Heather, a colored shawl would be too disrespectful? Black does not do anything for you." I was wearing my one decent mourning gown.

"We could say I don't have a black shawl."

"You are wearing a black shawl."

"Yes, but Fairfield would not have noticed."

"He does seem somewhat immune to ladies," she admitted.

Yet he had kissed my hand in Brighton, and gazed into my eyes. Where had his chivalry gone? Had he done it to con me into inviting him here?

"Perhaps Bunny will get an offer. They hit it off uncommonly well." On the way upstairs, I asked Thumm if Fairfield's servants were having their dinner now, for I did not want to run into his valet.

"They are making merry in the kitchen, Miss Hume," he said.

I ran upstairs, and hastened along to the Gold Suite. It was not locked. I closed the door quietly behind me. There was still sufficient light that lamps were not necessary. Fairfield had brought such a superfluity of toilet articles and clothes with him that it made searching difficult. The toilet table was littered with half a dozen unsuccessful cravats, along with a handsome array of brushes, comb, shoehorn, little lady's hand mirror—what on earth did he need that for?—toilet water, shaving paraphernalia, nail clippers, and suede nail-polishing brush with a horn back.

The clothespress was jammed tight with jackets, trousers, evening slippers, Hessians, top boots, and a pair of hand-knitted bedroom slippers. I quickly searched through the pockets of the clothing, again encountering a bewildering array of items, including a deal of money. Whole jingling bunches of guineas and shillings. This was a strange way of being dipped!

My hopes rose on those frequent occasions when my hand touched paper, but it was only invitations, bills, and one billet-doux from someone called Emerald, who spelled Knightsbridge as "nites bridje" and wrote of her "tru luv." A lightskirt, I deduced.

I looked under the bed, under the pillow and mattress, and in desperation in the toes of his various boots and slippers. I looked in every drawer and cranny of both chambers, and finally concluded that if Lord Fairfield carried any clues, he carried them on his person. I must try to create an opportunity to get him to take off his clothes. Poor Lord Fairfield would be inundated with wine or tea before the night was over.

I was just racing for the stairs when I remembered that I was to change my shawl. I exchanged my black cashmere for a pretty paisley patterned in rose and blue, and returned below. I need not have hurried. Bunny did his job well. We waited another half hour before the gentlemen joined us. Aunt Lovatt was becoming quite restless. If Fairfield noticed I wore a prettier shawl, he did not say so. As we dined at country hours, there was still a long evening to be filled with some entertainment for our guest.

There was only one entertainment worthy of the name where Mrs. Lovatt is concerned. She likes a "square game," which means cards for four. She will tolerate piquet for two in a pinch, but her first and last love is whist. She had not had a game since Papa's death, and was suffering for the lack of it.

"I cannot think a little square game in the privacy of our own home is ineligible, even when we are in mourning," she said, squinting to see if Fairfield was scandalized.

"A shilling a point?" he suggested. "As ladies are present, I do not suggest playing for real money." A shilling a point was pretty real to us. We usually played for pennies.

"We play for chicken stakes," Bunny told him. "Pennies."

"Ah." The paltry stakes did not diminish Fairfield's interest one iota. He didn't wait to call a servant, but helped Bunny set up the green baize table himself and drew forward the chairs.

Just as we began to take our seats, Bunny threw a spanner into the works. "I must be running along now. Enjoy your game, folks."

"Running along!" Mrs. Lovatt howled. "But we need you for the fourth, Mr. Smythe."

"Thing is, the Parish Council is meeting tonight. Shan't be long," he said, directing this reassurance to me. "Unless old Ned Firth gets the bit between his teeth and insists on discussing raising the rates again. But I shall be back by eleven." His tone gave an awful significance to the hour, and again he stared at me. I nodded, in hopes that he would stop these pointed looks.

"Must you go?" Mrs. Lovatt asked. The parish meetings were held in Hythe. Just getting there and back would take long enough. She would have said a deal more if not for our guest, who was smiling dimly at Bunny's desertion.

" 'Fraid I must. Can't let old Firth ram through a rise in our rates." This possibility was almost as bad as missing her game.

Lord Fairfield came to the rescue in an unforeseen way. "We could ask Kerwood to make a fourth. He is a famous dab at cards."

"Kerwood?" she asked with interest. "Is that your valet, milord? We often ask Mrs. Gibbons to make up a fourth, but she is not very sharp, poor soul."

Fairfield blinked. "I meant Kerwood Snoad," he said.

"Snoad!" she said, horrified. "No, no. I shall call for Mrs. Gibbons."

"He often made up a fourth at Branksome Hall,

when the duchess was short a player," Fairfield added blandly. "She spoke highly of his skill."

I watched as Mrs. Lovatt mentally dealt with this problem. In her opinion, outside of having a title or a Royal Pavilion, the finest adornment a person could have was skill with the cards. The table was out, the chairs arranged. And Snoad had the added respectability of having played with the duchess.

"If you think he would do, then by all means, let us ask Snoad down," she said.

She summoned Thumm to deliver the request, which sounded very much like an order, and we waited. After ten minutes, I was beginning to wonder if Snoad meant to decline our offer. It would not have surprised me a bit, until I remembered his love of titles. He had fawned disgustingly over Fairfield. He would come; he was just making himself decent. I felt an arrow of pity for the man. He certainly would not possess evening clothes. We ought to have told him his good jacket would do.

"What is keeping him?" Mrs. Lovatt demanded, shuffling the cards. In her eagerness for the game, she was like a deb waiting for her first date.

"Here he is now," Fairfield said.

I looked to the door, and felt a wave of relief. He looked all right, insofar as his habiliments went. He was not wearing evening clothes, but a good blue jacket and pantaloons that I had not seen before. His jacket fit him superbly. His raven hair was brushed to a gloss, and his cravat carefully arranged. I noticed that while he might have begged Papa's boots, he possessed a pair of well-polished Hessians. Actually, they were larger than Papa's boots. I wondered what master had given him this pair of too large castoffs. It seemed a pity that such a well-set-up man should have to wear hand-me-downs, but Snoad's impassive face showed nothing of his feelings.

"You look very nice, Snoad," my aunt exclaimed in surprise.

Snoad bowed punctiliously. "It is very kind of you to have me down, Mrs. Lovatt. Shall we begin?" He glanced at me as he took his seat. I detected a little smile at the corner of his lips. And worse, a little gold pigeon fob hanging at the end of his watch chain. If Auntie should spy it, she would probably accuse Snoad of theft, and I would have to admit having given it to him.

I knew, although she had not said so, that my aunt's idea was to partner Snoad herself, and let me have the honor of partnering Fairfield. The vacant chair was across from me, however, and it was there that Snoad sat. She had waited long enough. Without further ado, she began to deal. The last card turned up diamonds. "Diamonds are trump," she said, and picked up her hand.

"An excellent hand!" Fairfield exclaimed, rummaging through his cards. "Three trump cards!" The angle at which he held them made it perfectly possible for everyone at the table to see what he held.

Any revealing of a single card was anathema to my aunt. Cards were not so much a game to her as a war. "Best hold up your cards, Lord Fairfield. We do not want to give the competition any advantage," she said sharply.

He obediently tightened his grip on the cardboards. The game began. "I was just telling the ladies, Kerwood, that you used to play at Branksome Hall with the duchess."

"Yes, when her table was short," he said briefly. There had descended on his face the same tense look that I was accustomed to seeing on Auntie's during a game. It was obvious that he had no interest in chatter.

"I like a good game of whist," Fairfield continued. "Mind you, I prefer faro."

"Faro!" Mrs. Lovatt sneered. "There is no skill in that! It is merely guessing which card will turn up."

"And betting on it," Fairfield added. Obviously the wager was the thing with him.

"You have played a spade on my diamond, Lord Fairfield," Mrs. Lovatt said a little later. "You cannot be out of trumps so soon, since you informed us you have three."

"By Jove! You're right." He redeemed his spade and tossed a king on Auntie's ace.

She stared at him as if he were mad. If he had three diamonds, he ought not to have played this high one on her ace. She bit her lips, but said nothing. Fairfield did more than enough talking for us all.

The game proceeded, with Fairfield reneging, revoking, and trumping his partner's tricks at every turn of the hand. My eyes kept turning hypnotically to the little dangling gold pigeon. I wished Snoad would tuck it into his pocket. Snoad said very little, but I saw the laughter brimming behind his polite facade every time Fairfield made a faux pas. Meanwhile, Snoad and I won the first rubber.

"Perhaps if we concentrated a little on the game, instead of discussing how much you lost at faro, Lord Fairfield, we might manage to make a few tricks next time," my aunt said through thin lips.

She was nearly as annoyed at his ignoring me as at his awful playing. I could forgive him the former. He did not know his duty was to flirt with me. "What hour is it getting to be?"

Snoad reached for his watch. "Only nine-thirty," I said, before he pulled it out. I believe he heard the panic in my tone, for while he had his hand at his vest, he tucked the pigeon into his pocket, and I could relax.

"A glass of wine will brighten us all up," Fairfield said, and went to fetch the bottle himself.

"Let us hope so!" my aunt said grimly.

The next rubber was equally disastrous for Auntie and Fairfield. While Fairfield fell in her esteem, Snoad rose higher. He had a keen eye for any advantage, and played to win. He made a few sensible comments, but did not prattle. Her tight-lipped "Well done, Snoad," of the first rubber had become "Well played, Mr. Snoad," by the second.

When the game was finished and the winnings handed to Snoad and myself, my aunt gave Snoad the ultimate compliment. "We must have another hand one evening," she said, examining him minutely.

Snoad inclined his head and replied with a winning smile, "Let us arrange to be partners, ma'am, and we'll take any pair you care to invite. You play a challenging game."

"And under a severe handicap," she was betrayed into saying, shooting a wicked look at her partner.

Snoad overcame his love of nobility to the extent of saying good night and leaving as soon as the game was over. "I usually check out the loft before retiring," he said. "It has been a most enjoyable evening."

I wanted a word alone with him, and used loft business as an excuse. "I shall send a boy up tomorrow," I said, walking him toward the door.

When we were beyond earshot, he said, "Can I take it out now?"

"I didn't tell my aunt I had given away Papa's watch," I said, feeling like a fool. "I was afraid it might upset her."

"I thought as much. I treasure it the more, knowing it is our secret." His smile was warm, when there was every reason that he might have been angry at such a troublesome gift. That, I felt, was the mark of a gentleman.

I knew a snack would be served before retiring, and was rather hoping Auntie would invite him to return. It would not take more than another game of cards before even that honor was extended to him, for he had certainly been on his best behavior. Other than our parting words, I might as well have been another gentleman, for any special interest he paid me. And my nose was a little out of joint.

The snack arrived as soon as Snoad left. I was keeping an eye on the clock, and knew that the assignation with Depew was drawing close.

As soon as the tea was poured and the sandwiches passed, Mrs. Lovatt said to Fairfield, "You have met Snoad before, I assume, as you called him Kerwood. I didn't know that was his name."

"That is what they called him at Branksome Hall. He was a great favorite there."

"Why was that? Had the duchess no children of her own?"

"Half a dozen of them. Three sons. There is Mait-

131

land, the heir, and Willie, a son in the Peninsula, and a younger one, along with three daughters. They are married and scattered about here and there."

This gave the duchess the age Snoad had claimed, and the dispersement of the daughters also matched his story. He had told the truth about that at least.

"Kerwood saved the heir's life, it seems," Fairfield continued. "Dove into the lake and saved him when his boat capsized. Nothing was too good for Kerwood after that. His father was their gamekeeper, but the duchess had Snoad educated at the vicarage, to pay him for saving her son's life."

"A pity he hasn't done more with his education. He is very gentlemanly. He seems a bright lad, and personable. I know Harold, my brother, had a good opinion of him."

I listened closely to all this, for, of course, I had my own interest in Snoad. I knew what use he was putting his cleverness and his personableness to—spying for the French!

Bunny has a way of showing up when there is food on the table. He arrived while we were eating, and gobbled up what was left of the sandwiches and cakes. His imperative glances at the clock kept me alert to the passing of time. My aunt asked him about the parish rates, and he assured her the increase had not passed.

At five to eleven I began stifling imaginary yawns. Fairfield, who was a gentleman, even if he was a bit of a fool, took the hint and suggested it was time to retire.

"You run along, too, Auntie," I said. "I'll see that Thumm locks up."

She went upstairs with Fairfield, trying to be polite to make up for her short temper over the baize table. As soon as they were out of sight, Bunny and I ran out the east door to meet Depew by the blasted pine.

Chapter Eleven

It was a clear night, so clear we actually caught a glimpse of the moon's face, floating in the black sky high above. In my excited state, I felt the moon was smiling. All my recent duties having to do with Papa's death and funeral had been sad, and sometimes onerous, but here was a duty that gave only pleasure. What could be more delightful than to be meeting a spy by moonlight, to keep England safe and bring rogues to justice?

We ran straight to the blasted pine. Depew was not in sight at first, but when he recognized our voices, he appeared, wraithlike, from behind another tree. "Were you seen leaving?" he demanded in a low tone.

While Bunny assured him we were not Johnnie Raws, I examined our mentor in hopes that he might provide some romance, to put the cap on this daring enterprise. Alas, he was no more handsome than on first acquaintance. Unless he could transform himself by actually saving my life in some heroic manner, there seemed little hope of turning him into a hero.

Depew inquired how we had spent the evening, and what we had discovered. I told him what had passed—the fruitless search of Fairfield's room, the coded verse found in the loft. I also mentioned those areas where I sensed some shortcoming in his own methods. He accepted my criticism mildly.

"We are only mortal men, Miss Hume," he admitted. "We err, like everyone else. Perhaps my greatest error was in not fully trusting you." I gave him a sharp look. "But your enthusiasm for the job has convinced me to take you fully into my confidence. I have a special job for you."

My heart raced. Bunny caught my eye, and though we tried to look unmoved, I knew he wanted to shout, and so did I. "What job is that?" Bunny inquired.

"London is desperate to recover the code book. We gave your father one, for coding the messages he sent for us."

"Surely Snoad has found the book. He was writing that coded poem," I said.

"That is not the code. Snoad must have a ladybird he corresponds with. It is not a rhymed code. I believe it consists of discrete letters and numbers."

"Are you sure my father had it? Perhaps they sent the messages to him already coded."

"No, he had to be able to both read the messages from abroad, and send the proper answer to suit the occasion. The alternatives would be given to him in advance. If the French are advancing, then x. If retreating, then y."

"But Snoad has been searching. He must have the book by now," I warned him.

"It is my hope that your father took great pains in its concealment. It is small, a little black leather-covered book only two inches by three, with no title on the cover. Only twelve of them are in existence. Your father was told to keep it concealed in a safe place, and to show it to no one."

"That's what Snoad's been looking for in Papa's study!" I exclaimed. "He *does* know about it, and he broke the outer door open himself, so we would think it was an intruder from outside."

"You just might be right about that break-in. I'll tell you one thing. I had your house under surveillance the whole time, and no one got in from outside. Since you tell me he also took your father's pistol, you must exercize extreme caution in your dealings with him."

"I think you ought to arrest him and search him and his belongings, Mr. Depew."

"Martin!" he reminded me. "I would prefer not to. Snoad is only a minor link in the chain of spies who infest England. With luck, and a little rope, he might lead us to other members."

"But if he has the code book, he might be sending false messages, and do irreparable harm."

"I have reason to believe he does not have it."

"What reason?" I asked, full of interest.

He scowled in displeasure at my persistence, but finally replied, "Because he is still looking. Last night I saw from outside a light moving about downstairs."

"Did you hear anything, Bunny? Mr. Smythe is sleeping in Papa's study," I explained to Depew.

"Not a sound," Bunny said.

"These men are professionals. They could walk over eggs without cracking one. I assume he would not have been performing a systematic search of the house if he had found it. We must lure him out, and hope he leads us to his henchmen."

"He doesn't go out much," Bunny said with a tsk of dismay.

"He asked this very day if he might have an assistant," I said in a hollow voice. "Very likely what he wanted was someone to watch the loft, so he could go out more."

"Arrange for him to have an assistant as soon as possible," Depew ordered.

"Funny he didn't use it as an excuse to bring in a man of his own," Bunny said.

Depew scowled. I was beginning to understand that he did not like having his actions questioned. "He could hardly bring in a servant with a French accent," he said sharply.

"I have already agreed to providing an assistant. It will be difficult to get the code book," I said, racking my brain to devise a scheme. "I'll listen at doors. If I overhear Fairfield and Snoad talking, then—"

"No!" I could see Depew was surprised at how his voice rang on the still night air. He looked around, and continued in a lower tone. "I don't want you to take any chances, Miss Hume. If they should overhear you, and pull you into the room . . ." He nodded his head in a way that expressed certain death, possibly preceded by a fate worse than death.

"A man's job. I'll do it," Bunny said, in that unwittingly arrogant way that men, even such tame fellows as Bunny, sometimes adopt toward ladies.

"There's no point listening at keyholes," Depew said. "They'll not discuss it. A quiet and thorough search when they are out is your best hope. Meanwhile, I have arranged that London send no messages of any import here. What would make more sense is to get them out of the house as soon as possible. We must draw them off to someplace a mile or so removed from Gracefield. Have you any idea how that might be accomplished?"

"It would be no problem getting Fairfield out. I could go driving with him, and let Bunny look around, but Snoad is another matter."

"I would rather you not have too much to do with Fairfield," Depew said, in a kindly way. "He plays the fool well, but that is not to say he is one. He uses that role to divert suspicion from his activities."

I found myself gaining a new respect for Fairfield, but this did not lessen my appreciation of Snoad's wits. "Which of them would be in charge? Is Snoad under Fairfield's supervision?"

"I wish I knew. Fairfield is a dark horse. A new man in the game."

"The birds have to be driven to spots some miles from the house and let loose, to teach them to fly home, as I explained in my letter," I said. "Papa often had Snoad do that. Perhaps that is why Snoad needs a helper."

"This shows definite promise," Depew said, smiling in approval. "You are the mistress of Gracefield, Miss Hume. Express your concern that the birds are not getting their training. Encourage Snoad to arrange a long flight. If you could get Fairfield to accompany him, and let me know where they are going . . ."

"Will you come into Gracefield and help us look?" I asked.

"No, that will be your job. I'll follow the men.

The birds, I assume, can be released from any direction. It is logical that Snoad would use this opportunity to meet with his cohorts. You may be sure he has spies set about the area, bringing any news picked up from our troops in the neighborhood. I may round up the whole crew. Or should I say, *we* may round up the whole crew? You are performing an extremely valuable service." He bowed to Bunny and myself.

We murmured our delight at the opportunity.

"I wish I could promise you a tangible reward, but the fact is, until this beastly war is over, you will be unsung heroes, your fame known only to a few top men in London. But after the war . . ."

Visions of titles danced before us. Dame Heather Hume might even become Lady Hume if we rounded up the entire crew.

We left, with promises to meet again by moonlight the next night. Bunny was to dash a message off to Mr. Martin at the inn the instant we could arrange for Snoad, and hopefully Lord Fairfield, to drive off together.

There was little more we could do that night, but we were too excited to just calmly go to bed. We walked down to the cliff that overlooks the sea, and stood gazing at the calm water. From below, a sound of footsteps rose on the still air. We crept closer, crouching to hide ourselves in case the intruder looked up.

It was one lone man, bundled up in a dark coat and muffler. He wore a cap pulled low over his eyes, of the sort the local fishermen wear. Gathering seafood from the shore has not the same odium as poaching. As the man carried a container of some sort, I thought he was looking for winkles or mussels, except that his eyes more often turned to Gracefield than to the beach.

As we stood watching, the man made a movement, and a light flashed from his dark lantern. He slid the covering back and forth three times in quick succession. The light flashed, up toward the loft.

"It's a message to Snoad!" I breathed in Bunny's ear.

"And Snoad's answering!" Bunny whispered. Three answering flashes came from the bartizan.

"Maybe they're going to meet!" The intruder sat down to wait, which seemed as if I had guessed right. "Do you have your pistol?"

"No. I'll get it." Bunny sheared off toward the east door before I could stop him.

If he did not meet Snoad coming out, it would be a miracle. I looked toward the bartizan for more signals. There were none. What I saw instead was a rope being let out from the bartizan, and soon a dark form began descending the rope. Snoad—I knew it was Snoad—came darting down like a monkey, bracing his feet against the walls of the house to aid his descent. My heart rose to my throat. Almost before I had time to be afraid, he was on the ground, darting toward the intruder on the beach.

The intruder rose and went to meet him. I edged along closer to overhear them. If a French accent came out of either mouth, I would know I had found another member of Snoad's gang.

"She be a hearty brew this time, sir," a rough voice said. A rough, very English voice. "None o' your doping with carmel syrup. Pure gold, and hot off the vessel." He handed Snoad a jug of what could only be smuggled brandy. "Try her."

Snoad pulled the cork and lifted the bottle to his lips. "Excellent, as usual, Trucker."

"Will this be the last one, since the great gaffer is done and gone?"

It was Papa who customarily bought this illicit brew! I ought not to have been surprised. Auntie said he let them use his beach, but I imagined this had been long ago.

Some gold coin chinked into the man's outstretched palm. "Let us continue the arrangement until further notice. I have a friend who would like a hogshead to take to London as well. Can you put one in Hume's stable? You'll find the payment lodged under the driver's seat of Lord Fairfield's rig."

"I know the rig. I seen the fancy gold on the door as it bowled along here. A hogshead it is, thankee, sir. I'll be back next fortnight then, as usual."

Trucker trudged off, and Snoad recorked the bottle, put it under his arm, and turned back to Gracefield.

I stayed crouched out of sight, happy to be rid of him, and with no notion of intervening, as tonight's crime was a relatively harmless one. Bunny chose that inauspicious moment to come bolting out of the east door, brandishing his pistol. Snoad saw him and stopped in his tracks.

"Is that you, Mr. Smythe?" he called. "No need to shoot. It's only Trucker making his rounds."

"Trucker, you say?" Bunny asked, smiling. "By Jove, I am fresh out. Mama gave the vicar my last jug. I'll have a word with him."

He ran off after Trucker, while I stood, staring in disbelief. I did not realize I had stood up straight until Snoad glanced over and saw me. "You are out late, Miss Hume," he said. And I, like a ninny, felt obliged to find an excuse.

"The night is so fine...."

"Yes, a nice evening for a climb," he replied, and returned to scamper up his rope to the loft. He had attached the jug of brandy to his waist in some manner, which did not appear to interfere with his climbing.

Bunny returned, his pistol in his waistband. "Trucker will put my bottle in the stable when he delivers Fairfield's. Well, that was all a hum, Heather, but not a complete waste. Trucker has the best brew on the coast. We might as well go in."

"I hope we have not alerted Snoad that we are on the lookout."

"He knows I am on the lookout for burglars. Won't make a thing of it."

I could hardly unbraid Bunny or Snoad when my own father had been involved in buying smuggled brandy. The incident left me on edge. I was not ready for bed, and suggested we listen at keyholes, despite Depew's warning. We went back indoors, and with Bunny to protect me, I tiptoed down the hall to Fairfield's room. He was chatting to his valet, but the subject was not a code book, or anything interesting. He was complaining about a spot on his jacket, and sounded quite as inane as ever. I remembered that I had not managed to spill wine on him, to make an opportunity to search his jacket for clues.

Now I knew at least what I was looking for. If Fairfield's dimness was a disguise, he might have the book, but Snoad had been here longer. He had searched Papa's office, and I still felt Snoad was the wilier man. I felt in my bones that Snoad had found the book by now, whatever Depew said. He had had all the time we were in Brighton to look for it. If either Snoad or Fairfield had the book, where would he carry it but safely on his person? It was not the loft or the house we should be searching, but Snoad's and Fairfield's pockets.

I mentioned this to Bunny when we had crept away from Fairfield's room. "After we break this ring of spies, I mean to go up to London and offer my services on a full-time basis," he said. "Mean to say, I ain't no wizard, but I ain't any stupider than Depew. Er, Martin. They have certainly got the book by now."

"A good idea, Bunny. Now, how could we search them? I think we must push them into the sea—oh, accidentally, of course, so they don't suspect anything. Then we'll help them remove their wet jackets, and rifle the pockets while they are being wrapped in a blanket."

"Might be in their trouser pockets," he said.

"Then they'll have to remove their trousers, too."

Chapter Twelve

An opportunity to dip Fairfield in the sea came the next morning after breakfast. All visitors who do not live on the coast want to have a walk along the shore to commune with nature, and comment that they only remember England is an island when they are on the coast. Otherwise, they go for years on end without ever thinking of it.

I offered to accompany Fairfield. I brought along a blanket, ostensibly in case we wanted to sit and watch the waves after he was tired of walking. Of course, my real reason was to have it handy when he "fell" into the sea. It would make removing his jacket more plausible.

Bunny rose to accompany us. That is where we came a cropper. Auntie, sensing a romance, wanted to leave me alone with Fairfield. She asked Bunny if he would mind taking a look at the wheels of the carriage. She imagined one was wobbling on our return from Brighton. There is little dearer to Bunny's heart than messing about with horses and carriages. Throw in a bottle of brandy to be recovered, and he went along, as happy as a pig in mire.

"Shall we go along to have a look at the ocean?" Fairfield said. I could think of no excuse to refuse, and went with him. My aunt would have been delighted with the trip. Fairfield was as gallant as can be. He leapt down the cliff like a gazelle, and caught me in his arms as I slid down.

The shingle beach was not easy walking in slippers. I saw that tipping Fairfield into the sea was not going to be an easy affair. There was some possibility that I would get wet myself, for he decided to hold my hand.

"It is the strangest thing," he said, "but you know, I go for months at a time without ever remembering that England is an island."

"I believe you mentioned your estates are all landlocked."

"Every one of them," he said, with a tone of pique.

"Pity."

I happened to glance up, and detected a form at the meshing of the loft. Snoad was watching us. He had removed the rope that spoke of last night's escapade. When Fairfield began to step up the courting, I became especially conscious of Snoad's dark eyes peering down. Fairfield chose the most worn-out technique imaginable to court me. He decided to teach me how to skip flat stones. Half a dozen gentlemen have tried to teach me this useless skill over the years. Perhaps if I had any interest in learning, I would have mastered it by now. As it lent some possibility of inundating Fairfield, however, I let him put his arm around me and guide my hand in the proper manner.

The trick, in the unlikely case that you are interested, is to twist the hand at an uncomfortable angle as close to parallel with the water as possible, so that the stone approaches the surface at a very acute angle. Otherwise, it merely sinks into the sea on contact. After several playful attempts and much body contact, Fairfield began to step up the flirtation.

One arm was already around my shoulder, one hand holding my right wrist. He put the other arm around me and pulled me into his arms to try for a kiss. It was the best opportunity I was likely to have, and my only regret was that Bunny was not there to assist me. I pulled myself free, at the same time shoving him as hard as possible toward the sea. It was sheer blind luck that he collided with a largish boulder and went sprawling on the wet shingle. A kindly wave chose that moment to crest and flow over him, wetting him quite thoroughly from the shoulders down. He held his head up, spluttering.

I was immediately all contrite and solicitous. "Oh, Lord Fairfield! I am so sorry! Let me help you up." He stretched out his hand, but it was his face that I looked at. I never saw such a murderous expression in my life. It was easy to believe Depew's warning that this was a clever fiend.

"Entirely my own fault," he said, through gritted teeth. My safety was in the balance for a second. He fought with the urge to pull me down beside him for a dunking, but his breeding got the better of him.

"We must get you out of those freezing clothes. Fortunately, I brought a blanket."

I began stripping him of his jacket. I felt the pockets while he wrapped himself, shivering, in the blanket. They held an assortment of junk, but there was no rectangle two inches by three. I carried the jacket, to allow Fairfield both hands to hold his blanket in place. As we hastened houseward, water squelching in his handsome top boots, I chanced to glance up to the loft. Snoad's shoulders were heaving in laughter. I ignored him and headed Fairfield to the east door, to keep the water out of the front hall.

Bunny was just coming from the stable, carrying his jug of brandy, wrapped in a paper that didn't fool anyone. "Lord Fairfield fell into the sea," I explained. "I have his jacket here, Bunny. Perhaps you can help him out of his boots and trousers in the shed. He won't want to trail water all through the house." My commanding eye told him what he was to do with the trousers.

He understood me at once. He gave me his brandy, and he assisted Fairfield into a sort of shed attached to the east door. I ran off to hide the brandy in Papa's office, to call Fairfield's valet, and to give a mendacious account of the outing to my aunt.

"Fairfield was standing on the big boulder and slipped," I said.

"That water is frigid! I hope he doesn't take a chill. On the other hand, that would prolong his visit," she said, smiling. "Still, we had best call for a hot bath, Heather."

When I met with Bunny later, I learned his search of the trousers had been fruitless. "Snoad must have the code book," I said. I knew in my bones Snoad would not be so easily drenched. He would not have hesitated to pull me into the water.

The "accident" threw a damper on my romance with Fairfield. Auntie thought him very toplofty to be so cool with us when the drenching was his own fault, and I, perforce, agreed with her.

"That is not to say he is not an excellent parti," she reminded me.

"He makes a very unsatisfactory fourth at whist," I mentioned, to tease her.

"An annual Season in London would more than make up for it, as you are no lover of the cards," she replied. "I hope he does not take into his head to play again tonight. Such a pity he has not got Snoad's skill, or that Snoad has not Fairfield's eligibility. But that is always the way. You can't have everything in a man."

"All things considered, I think I prefer Snoad," I said, to vex her.

"A lady takes her coloring from her husband, Heather. I think you would prefer to be blue than black."

"Why do you call him black?" I asked, curious. I thought she meant his character.

"Why, his shiny black hair, and those dark eyes, to be sure." She cast a worried frown at me, and I knew that even Auntie recognized him for a charmer. "Looks fade. Money and titles last," she said firmly. Then added less firmly, "Mind you, I was surprised he is so gentlemanly, and such a good hand at whist."

For myself, a skill at whist rated very low. Yet despite the obvious disparity in their social standing, I still felt Snoad would provide the more interesting partner. I shook myself back to reality. They were both traitors! And I would see both of them led off to London in chains before this case was finished.

Chapter Thirteen

I spoke to the backhouse boy about assisting Snoad in the loft. Cassidy was thrilled to death to be relieved of the onerous duty of chopping wood and carrying coal. Even when I pointed out that he would still have to perform these duties during half the day, he continued happy.

"It might turn into a regular thing, though," he said, smiling from ear to ear. Cassidy was young, only fourteen, but a bright lad. "I'm good with birds, miss. Cook always has me collect the eggs. She says I have a gentle hand."

"Go up and ask Snoad what hours he will want you, and arrange with Mrs. Gibbons how much wood and coal she will need before you go."

Lunch was a subdued affair. When it was over, I asked Lord Fairfield if he would like to go up to the loft, to begin making his selection of birds. He agreed. Bunny tagged along to protect me. Cassidy was already at work, filling the water pans for the pigeons, and sweeping the floor. I could not believe he had got such a bargain as he thought.

Snoad was scribbling something in a book. I caught a glance at it, but it was only Papa's account book, in which he was making entries having to do with the birds' progress. He immediately set the book aside and came toward us. His smirk called to mind Fairfield's dunking. He bowed to me, then addressed himself to Fairfield.

"Milord, I am happy to see you did not take a chill. An unfortunate accident. One must be wary on the shingle beach. It is slippery when wet."

"No harm done, except to my jacket—and my pride," Fairfield said, with a forgiving grin in my direction.

"I thought Lord Fairfield might want to begin making his selection of birds," I said, glancing around. "He is particularly interested in Caesar and Cleo's birds. Ah, I see Caesar is back." Cleo fluttered around the branch excitedly.

He sat in his tree, staring down at his inferiors. Caesar is a large bird. His cere is black, which gives him a scowling look. His color is undistinguished, a pearly gray with a purplish breast and some black on his wings. What sets him apart in looks is a distinguishing set of neck feathers. They curve forward, forming a sort of snood behind his head.

"Caesar is back!" Fairfield exclaimed. I had an impression, just from the corner of my eye, that Snoad gave him an admonishing look. Fairfield examined Caesar. "Good lord! What an odd-looking fellow he is. He seems a bit perturbed about something." He was indeed spreading his wings and squawking, but not moving from his perch at all.

"He is mostly rock pigeon, but partly jacobin," Snoad explained. "It is the latter that accounts for his hood. And the lady beside him is the missus, Cleo." She preened her white feathers, then pecked angrily at her beloved. I saw that pigeons, while monogamous, were not necessarily always in harmony. "The splash of burgundy on her chest is unique in our birds," Snoad mentioned.

Fairfield went forward to admire them, but Snoad said that as they seemed upset, he would show our guest Sextus and Aurelia instead. "This is the pair you are interested in," he said, and added in an accusing way, "If Miss Hume plans to sell them, that is. I am trying to convince her to keep them. Their training has just begun. It might already be too late to move them."

I rushed in to execute Depew's orders. "I am somewhat concerned about the training, Snoad. I have not seen you taking the birds from the nest to have them fly home."

"That is why I asked for an assistant. I plan to go afield this afternoon. I am a little concerned that the lad you sent is old enough to make sure they are all back, and to time their return."

"Cassidy is fourteen. He knows how to count and tell the time. Where will you take them?"

"I had planned to drive north of Atherton."

"Perhaps Lord Fairfield would like to accompany you," I suggested.

Snoad looked quite astonished at my suggestion. "If you are sure you wish to part with him," he said, in a brash tone that a servant has no right to use with his employer.

"I have several letters to write to friends, thanking them for their condolences over my father's death."

"It sounds a dandy outing," Fairfield said at once. "But why don't we drive to Dover? Along the sea would be a more interesting drive, and I have relatives there. I haven't been to Dover in a dog's age."

"The birds have been to Dover many times. They have to fly from all directions," Snoad replied.

"Of course," Fairfield said, though I believe even this basic fact of training was unknown to him. "What time shall we leave?"

"No time like the present," Snoad replied.

"Shall we take my rig? Sixteen miles an hour," Fairfield tempted.

Snoad's lips stretched in appreciation. "If you don't mind having it encumbered with pigeon cages," he replied.

Bunny and I made a hasty exit. I hoped the gathering and caging of the pigeons would take long enough for Bunny to gallop to the inn and notify Depew of their destination.

"Did you notice his trick?" Bunny asked, with an air of excitement.

"What do you mean?"

"He had Caesar taped to his perch."

"Taped? What do you mean?"

"His claws were taped onto the branch."

"How very odd! Why would he do that?"

"Beats me."

"It cannot have anything to do with spying. I wish I knew more about the birds, but no doubt there is some reason for it. Cleo was not taped down."

Bunny posted off at once, and I took up a position

in the saloon that gave me a view of the others' departure. When Snoad and Fairfield passed the window, their friendly manner told me that they were working together. There was not a single whiff of the servant in Snoad's demeanor. In fact, it was Snoad who held the ribbons, and he handled the frisky grays very well, too.

I had very little hope of finding the code book, but I would look. To be rid of Cassidy while I did so, I told him the wood was getting low in the kitchen, and I would guard the loft till he returned. There were so many places to look that I despaired of finding it. There were all the cages, to begin with. Searching them was extremely unpleasant. Many of the birds were incubating eggs, and put up a great flurry when I intruded. The place was full of feathers by the time I finished, and, of course, there was no sign of the book.

I looked every place, all along the ledges of the roof, in Papa's account book, and in all the nooks and crannies. By the time Cassidy returned, the loft was ringing with the throaty sound of disturbed birds. I noticed that Caesar was no longer in the tree, and asked Cassidy about the taping.

"That was to keep him from Cleo while you was here, miss," he said, with a bold grin. I swallowed a grin at Snoad's idea of my prudishness, and thought no more of it.

"But what ails the birds, miss? What have you done?" Cassidy demanded. The squawking was quite noticeable.

"Nothing. A hawk has been flying past the screen and frightened them. You'd best sweep up these feathers."

I ran down one flight of stairs to Snoad's rooms. They were locked as before, which gave me hope that the book might be within. I got the key ring from my father's desk, and after several tries, found one big brass key that fit the lock. I entered, my insides quaking, and gazed around at a room that had been rigged out as a study.

I remembered the desk from a little-used bedroom. Other furnishings had been brought up, too. There was a fine blue bergère chair from another suite, bookcases, good lamps, a carpet, all the fixings of a polite chamber. Pretty good treatment for a servant! I spotted his bottle of brandy sequestered under the desk. I immediately rushed to the desk. It was not locked, which surprised me.

It held various accounts having to do with the feed and management of the pigeons. There wasn't a single private letter there. As I thought about that, it seemed odd. Snoad did occasionally receive letters, usually from Branksome Hall. His replies had also been seen from time to time on the salver in the hall downstairs, awaiting the post. He had no personal mementos, no pictures of mother or family framed on the desk, no bibelots in memory of a trip here or there.

One would think, from the looks of the room, that he had landed on earth the day he came to Gracefield. The lack of any personal items suggested concealment. Did all his personal memorabilia have a French accent, perhaps? I examined the books in the bookcase next. It was a big job, as I had to remove them one by one and look behind them, and also shake them in hope of finding notes concealed between their leaves.

I took note of the titles while I searched. There was a good sprinkling of novels and poetry, some of them from my father's library, but none of them in French. Others were books of geography or history. I read the flyleafs. Not one of them had his name inscribed, but several of them had had the blank page in front cut out with a razor.

I went into the next room, and observed with a jab of anger that it, too, held many items from guest rooms belowstairs. Why had my father given a servant such good furnishings? What I did *not* see was any sign of the scientific work that was the excuse for Snoad's second room. "A place for Snoad to do his scientific work," I remembered my father saying. I noticed that Snoad had had our journals brought upstairs for his perusal when we were finished with them. There were plenty of journals scattered about, giving the room a messy look.

I searched the room quickly. On the bedside table was the book of Byron's poetry he had been reading in the loft. A patent pen sat beside the book. I leafed through the volume and found the sheet with the poem. Another poem had been written on the bottom of the same page. It read:

>   As moon to sky
>   As water to sea
>   As blossom to meadow
>   Is my love to me.
>
>   As heather to hills
>   As dew to the morn
>   For now and for always

He had scratched out two or three last lines, apparently finding it difficult to rhyme "morn." There was a "torn" and a "born" in there, neither making much sense. What struck my eye, after a second reading, was that he had used the word "heather." Was that coincidence, or had he been thinking of me? I read the verse again, and felt a twinge of pity for Snoad. Had the poor fool gone falling in love with me? I supposed that even a spy was not immune to Cupid's shafts. Even a French spy. It softened my animosity to Snoad, but the facts were still there. He was the enemy. Even now he might be meeting his cohorts, planning the destruction of England.

I reread the first poem, disliking those "gray" eyes, when mine were green. Did he dash off a bit of doggerel to every lady he met? I finished searching the room, tidied everything up so he would not know I had been in, and left, locking the door behind me.

Then I went below to await Bunny's return. He came shortly after. "I told Depew. Offered to go with him, but he says to stay here and look for the book."

"I am certain Snoad has the book, and carries it on him. I searched the loft and his room."

"Seems to me Depew might need a hand, if Snoad is meeting his men."

"What did he say?"

"Said he'd handle it. Told me to come back here."

"I wish we had a more clever superior, Bunny. I am not at all sure Depew is smart enough to catch Snoad."

"He's been put in charge. He mustn't be as stupid as he seems. I mean to say, why was Snoad searching the house t'other night if he's found the book? It is Fairfield who is the raw one. A very shallow fellow. The deeper you dig with him, the shallower he gets. You ought to have heard him squawk about his ruined jacket when you dunked him."

"Let us look some more. We could try the cellar. Papa kept a close watch on his wine. He was usually downstairs twice a week."

That is how we wasted a fine afternoon, by searching the dank, cold cellar. Auntie demanded to know what we were about, and Bunny said we were taking an inventory of the bottles, to see if we should order more wine.

"You know Papa liked to keep well stocked," I added.

Auntie shook her head at this lunacy, but left us alone. Of course, we found nothing except dirt and cobwebs and black beetles. This undertaking made a bath necessary before dinner. I heard Fairfield and Snoad passing in the hall while I was in the tub. "It must have been an accident, Kerwood," I heard Fairfield say, in a loud voice.

"Accident be damned. We were followed," Snoad replied angrily. "Do you remember, Heather asked where we were going?"

"No, did she?"

So Snoad called me Heather behind my back, did he? And Fairfield, I feared, was every bit as stupid as I thought. He had not remembered that I asked their destination.

I was most eager to talk to Depew, and learn what "accident" had transpired on that trip to Atherton. Whatever it was, the spies had returned unharmed, and worse, alerted that they were under observation. I felt things could not go on much longer in this semipeaceful vein. They were drawing to a crisis. I remembered, too, that Snoad had Papa's pistol. Then I had to put on a smile and go down and join Fairfield for dinner, as though he were not a spy, here to trick us.

Chapter Fourteen

I was, of course, extremely curious to learn what "accident" had befallen Snoad and Fairfield during their trip. What first occurred to me was that Depew had rigged the curricle to break down, but a second thought showed me the ineligibility of that course. Depew wanted to see where they were going, and whom they were meeting. Besides, he didn't know what carriage they would be taking. I decided it was a genuine accident, which Snoad's guilty conscience turned into a plot. Spies would always have to be suspicious of everyone.

As Fairfield seemed fairly dim-witted, I hoped to find out from him that evening what sort of accident it was. As things turned out, the opportunity did not arise. He claimed a sick headache after dinner and remained in his room. I did have letters to write, and when Auntie suggested piquet, I was quick to remind her of them, and let Bunny be her partner. While we were setting up the table, I told him that I was going up to the loft. If I was not down in half an hour, he must come after me.

Depew wanted me to keep an eye on the loft, and I wanted to try if I could discover from Snoad what had happened that afternoon. With these frail excuses, I abandoned my partner to piquet and went upstairs. The loft was cool and quiet. A gentle cooing from the nests was the only sound. As my eyes grew accustomed to the darkness, I espied a form at the far end, near Caesar's tree. There was something menacing in it, hovering silently in the corner. It moved against the screen, and suddenly assumed the form of a man. Snoad.

My racing heart resumed its normal pace as he detached himself from the tree and advanced toward me. He was dressed in black, but not evening clothes. Instead of a jacket, he wore a thick knitted jersey against the wind.

"Good evening, Miss Hume," he said, bowing. "Are my services required at the whist table this evening?" His rich voice was edged in sarcasm.

To avoid a skirmish, I decided to conciliate him. "Not this evening, Snoad, but my aunt was favorably impressed with your skill. She liked you."

"I am, of course, vastly interested in your *aunt's* opinion," he replied flirtatiously.

I had not come to flirt. "Lord Fairfield is not feeling quite the thing this evening," I said. "Perhaps the outing was too much for him."

"I am sorry to hear it."

The man was an oyster. I could not ask outright if there had been an accident, or he would know I had been eavesdropping. "Mr. Smythe described him as a Corinthian. I had not thought one of those athletic gentlemen would be overcome by a drive to Atherton," I said leadingly.

"It was hardly a tiring drive for him. He was kind enough to let me handle the ribbons."

"That was generous of him. His team is valuable, I believe."

Snoad didn't answer. He crossed his arms and stared at me a moment. "I don't think you came up here to discuss Fairfield's headache," he said.

"No, I didn't."

"Why did you come?"

Necessity betrayed me into indiscretion. "I seem to recall I was asked to return. Soon, and often, I believe you said." It sounded like an invitation to flirtation, and Snoad was not tardy in reply."

A quizzical smile lit his face. "Ah, then it is a social visit!" he exclaimed. "Excellent. I have been pondering the eligibility of offering you a glass of your father's excellent sherry. As it is a social call, I expect some refreshment might be offered."

I was relieved he did not offer brandy, but he did not refer to last night's strange meeting at all. He went to the table between the two old mildewed chairs and began fiddling with wine and glasses. "How is Cassidy working out?" I inquired, to keep the conversation going, but on an impersonal subject.

"He has the makings of a good pigeon man. Gentle hands, and a true love of the birds. You chose wisely. *Salut!*" He touched his glass to mine, and we drank.

It was extraordinarily difficult to find a subject that did not involve either spying or flirtation. In desperation I said, "Has Fairfield selected his birds yet?"

"No. He seems more interested to learn how a proper operation is carried on. He is just beginning to assemble his flock. You have noticed his lack of expertise, I think?"

"Yes. I wonder how long he plans to stay. He mentioned a day or two, when the invitation was first extended."

"There are other attractions than the pigeons," he said. His black eyes studied me. I turned away to place my glass on the table. Snoad did the same.

My first mental response was amazement that he would mention their spying, even obliquely. In a twinkling I realized *I* was the alleged attraction. "Oh! Yes, he is an excellent parti, I believe."

"Which of his excellencies do you refer to? His title or his wealth?"

"Actually, it was his face and figure I meant. He is very handsome." It seemed ludicrous to be prating of Fairfield's beauty when the man beside me was a regular Adonis. It was like comparing a candle to the sun.

"I had not thought Miss Hume would settle for a handsome face and a broad set of shoulders," he scoffed.

"Well, throw in the title and estates..."

His voice, when he spoke, was rough with annoyance. "Do you really care so much for a title?"

"Not unduly, I hope, but there is some appeal in a tiara," I answered with a dismissing laugh.

Frustration steamed from his obsidian eyes. An ungentlemanly curse growled from the depths of his throat, and while I watched this jungle display in disbelieving fascination, his hand flashed out and gripped my wrist. He crushed me against the unyielding wall of his chest. My one yelp of outrage was silenced by his lips, which found mine with the swift, unerring accuracy of a hawk seizing its prey. I made one convulsive effort to escape. His arms tightened to bands of oak, clamping me to him. His angry growl softened to a reassuring croon, which was more devastating than those lips that flamed on mine, and the pressure of his strong body. Something inside me melted at the exquisite intimacy of that sound, coming from inside him.

Beneath the soft jersey, his back was strong and wide. I allowed myself the luxury of examining it. Snoad followed my example. His warm hands caressed my body with possessive knowledge, leaving a trail of fire where he took my measure. I gave up all hope of escape, or of wanting to, and abandoned myself to his primitive lovemaking. It was at once more physical, yet more metaphysical, than I had imagined it could be. Oh yes, I had imagined this scene a hundred times, yet for once, reality outpaced imagination. Like the beat of a drum, my heart throbbed, seeming to echo not only in my ears, but in my loins. It engendered a fever at the very core, robbing me of common sense.

The beating spread through me like wildfire, laying waste the last dregs of my self-control. I was overwhelmed by a yearning need for—something. I was at that point where the mind vaguely conceives of an unimagined infinity, a place beyond space and time, yet I was tethered to the here and now by his devouring embrace. I tried to turn away. His hand palmed my head, turned it back, and found my lips again.

Such rapture could not long be endured. With the seasoned art of the master, Snoad released me gently, slowly. His lips softened from demand to pleading; his arms lessened their tension, and too soon we stood an inch apart, gazing at each other like a pair of thieves.

While I hastily surveyed whether I should bridle up and deride him for this outrage, or throw myself back into his arms whimpering, as I felt like doing, Snoad gave his lower lip a sharp bite, and laughed. It was the sort of nervous eruption that crops out under mental stress. It told me nothing, except that he was ashamed of himself.

Having anticipated either an abject apology or a declaration of undying devotion, I was highly displeased with that laugh. I knew which course I must take: the bridling-up course.

"Is molesting unsuspecting ladies your idea of a joke, Snoad?" I demanded. "I find it as vulgar and reprehensible as everything else about you." These brave words were marred by a breathless voice. I wished I had kept my mouth shut until I was more fully recovered.

His black brows quirked up. "Unsuspecting?" he said. I glared him down. "I wasn't really laughing." He said it so simply and so contritely that I was sorry I had lashed out at him. "It was shock," he added. When he reached to take my hand, I let him. I wanted to feel his touch again. "It's a devil of a situation, isn't it, Heather? You cannot love Fairfield. I don't believe it. It's only the title you love."

"Of course I don't love him! But I could never marry you, Snoad. I must marry a *gentleman* at least." Not that he had asked me!

"Do you really care so much for birth?"

"You know this is impossible."

"I'd marry you if I were the king of England, and you a serving wench."

"Then you would have a revolution on your hands, sir, and in my opinion, you would deserve it."

"Then I'd make you my official mistress."

This idea was too dangerous to persue. "I shan't come up here again, Snoad." An arrow pierced my heart to consider my desolate future. Then I remembered Depew's orders. "Not without an escort," I added.

He lifted my hand to his lip and kissed it ardently. "Just come," he said softly. "Don't deprive me of even the sight of you. I couldn't endure it." While my heart was melting at that tender speech, he added, "And for God's sake, keep Fairfield away from the ocean. You can make me jealous from the east park. I can see you equally well under the elm trees. You don't want to drown the poor fool."

"People who spy are apt to see things they don't want to see," I said grandly, and left. How had I come to use that dangerous word "spy"? I turned and rushed downstairs, before any other unwise words were said, or unwise things done.

I went to my room to recover my wits. I was trembling. So this was why, and how, respectable ladies fell into alliances with their grooms or footmen. I would not be so swift to laugh at them another time. Such a powerfully compelling thing, this attraction between the sexes. It drove the hummingbird and the horse, the flea and the elephant. It drove Papa to Mrs. Mobley. I could understand it now, and to understand is to forgive. But I must not let this infatuation drive me to indiscretion. And that meant I must avoid being alone with Snoad. Kerwood. He had called me Heather, and I wished I had used his first name.

Snoad didn't suit him. It sounded like toad. What he required was a princess to turn him into a prince by her kiss. I glanced in the mirror, and was disgusted by the moonling smiling back at me. How could I so far forget duty as to go falling in love with a spy? Five minutes remained of the half hour that would bring Bunny to my rescue. I was about to return belowstairs when I heard Fairfield's door open.

Was he going to join us below? He might be more forthcoming about the "accident" that Snoad thought was no accident. What could it be? I listened, but his footsteps retreated instead of advancing toward my door, and the staircase. He was not going downstairs. There was only one place he could be going: to the loft.

I darted downstairs, and found Bunny just rising from the card table, using the excuse of a glass of wine. I poured it for him and said, "I'm going back up. Fairfield just went up to the loft."

"Learn anything?" he asked.

"No, but I'm going to listen at the door."

"Depew said not to."

"Depew is not God."

"Be careful. I'll check in half an hour if you're not down."

"All right." I said a few words to Auntie and left.

I stopped to tap at Fairfield's door, to make sure he had not returned. His valet replied. "I was just wondering if Lord Fairfield is feeling better," I said.

The valet raised his finger to his lips, while adjusting his shoulders to conceal the empty bed. "He's sleeping, miss. I gave him a few drops of laudanum half an hour ago. The best thing for toothache."

"I hope he feels better by morning."

The valet smiled and closed the door. He and Fairfield ought to have gotten together on his lordship's malady. Toothache indeed! Without wasting another moment, I went to the door up to the loft and began a silent, slow ascent. I was grateful for Fairfield's laxity. He had left the door open an inch. The men sat at the table, drinking Papa's sherry and smoking his cheroots. They spoke in tones just a notch lower than normal, which carried well on the still night air.

"She's got to be working with Depew," Snoad said. *She* was, of course, me. Or I, as the case may be. "She's rifled my room." How did he know that? I had been careful! "She told him where we were going this afternoon. And she came up here this evening trying to wheedle information out of me."

"How?"

"By the usual method of ladies, John. Her charms."

"Ah. You could tell her the truth."

Snoad laughed, a nasty laugh. "She wants to know when you're leaving, incidentally."

"When am I?"

I took note of this. It was Snoad who was in charge. And Snoad had tried to cozen me with his charms. The cozening was not all in one direction.

"I'm just waiting for word from Caesar. She suspects Caesar is being used, of course. She keeps asking about him. You nearly blew it when you showed your surprise at Caesar's return."

"It was his being in Caesar's tree that fooled me."

"And Heather. A pity Cleo dislikes Hector so

much. She didn't help, pecking at him. I told Cassidy I was taping him down to prevent a mating when Miss Hume came up. He thought it very civil of me."

My blood boiled to hear all this. I had been duped, made a fool of for days. Caesar was abroad, bringing in an important message.

"I'll send out the last message after Caesar arrives," Snoad said. "He should be here tonight, then we'll have to abandon this position."

"Where to next?"

"We'll receive our orders from headquarters. I'll be damned glad to get out of here, I can tell you. I mean to ask for something in London. More going on there."

London is swarming with spies, I remembered Depew had said.

"Seems to me there is plenty going on here. That little shoot-out this afternoon was lively. Perhaps I oughtn't to have winged him."

"A pity you didn't kill him," Snoad said ruthlessly.

So the "little accident" had been a pitched battle, using bullets. They must have spotted Depew, and tried to kill him. Such desperate goings-on as this were more than I had bargained for. I retreated back down the stairs before they caught me and put a bullet through me as well.

I was weak with fear, and went again to my room to recover. I reviewed their conversation. Caesar was on his way with a crucial message. That was why he had been missing, and why some other bird had been used to fool me. I had thought Caesar's hood unique in our loft, but obviously I was mistaken.

I could not sit idly by and let Snoad recover that message, and send out some false orders that might imperil our troops. I knew now that he had the code book. He had said point-blank that he would send out a message. I had to be rid of him, at once. The only thing I could think of was to relieve him of his post. This was my house; I paid him. I could order him to leave, and I would do so. I felt it imperative to consult with Depew on this matter first, however.

I went below, and by eye contact let Bunny know it was crucial that I speak to him. He began yawning and soon said, "I don't know about you, Mrs. Lovatt, but I am ready for the feather tick."

"It is early yet," she said, glancing at the clock. Piquet was not her real love, however. And Bunny was not her first choice of partner. She soon acceded. I was happy that she did not linger long behind, but went abovestairs to continue her rendezvous with Sir Walter Scott. She was greatly involved with his Waverley novels. She said they had helped her through her brother's death.

"What did you learn?" Bunny demanded as soon as we were alone.

I emptied my budget, and he listened, frowning in concentration. "I was right. The bird was taped to the tree," he told me, with a wise look.

"And they know Depew is an agent."

"That'd be why Depew is so hell-bent we not use his name, or let them catch a sight of him. He's not wearing his Horse Guards jacket, but that wouldn't fool them."

"You'd best go to the inn and speak to him."

"I'm gone. Don't tackle Snoad alone. I'll go up with you when you give him his marching papers."

"I am not that foolhardy. They tried to kill Depew this afternoon. Hurry back, Bunny. I am frightened out of my wits, harboring that pair of assassins."

I was sad, too, that my great love affair had fizzled out to nothing. What is it about rakes and ruthless men that we foolish ladies inevitably fall in love with them?

Chapter Fifteen

It was eleven o'clock before Bunny returned from the inn. "Depew's not there," he said.

"Did they say when he was expected to return? How badly was he hurt?"

"They hadn't seen him since noon. I tried the blasted pine. There's no message there either."

"He has men posted around the house. Perhaps one of them knows where he is. Or he might be there himself," I said, brightening at the possibility.

"Best have a look."

I snatched up a shawl and we went out together. A dense fog had rolled in from the sea. It hugged the ground in an impenetrable blanket, which lightened to rags of cloud above, but still made vision uncertain. The moon was reduced to a dull glow behind layers of mist. Every bush assumed the form of a man, every tree a giant. We went peering into the mist, calling softly. We had no fear that Depew's men would shoot us. They would know we were on the right side. One advantage of the fog was that it prevented Snoad from spotting us, if he chanced to glance down from the loft.

We circled the house, calling into the night, then made a larger circle, without encountering a single soul. "That is odd! He told us he was having the house watched at all times," I said. "Did the inn say when he would be back?"

"Not a word. He wasn't in. That's all they said."

"Fairfield said he had winged him. I hope it was not serious. Oh, Bunny, if he is dead—" My voice quavered.

"And Caesar bringing in a message tonight . . ."

"It is all on our shoulders now," I said, trying to rise to the occasion, and draw Bunny along with me, for his voice was also unsteady. "There is another thing. Snoad will send out a false reply to that message. It might mean the difference in winning or losing the war. We cannot let him do it."

We stood a moment, considering the unique and important role that Fate had assigned us, half proud of the honor, and half scared out of our wits.

"You'll have to turn Snoad off tonight," he said. "And Fairfield, too."

"What shall I tell Auntie?"

"May just have to tell her the truth—tomorrow."

"Do you have your pistol? We cannot go up there unarmed."

"Right here," he said, patting a bulge in his jacket.

I was shaking like an aspen in the wind when we returned to the house. We had a glass of wine to give us false courage, and while we drank, we discussed details of how to handle the situation.

"I shall take along a few footmen," I said.

"Can't. Depew don't want anyone to know what's going on. We'll continue to follow his plan, do the thing right. Mean to say, we want to go on using Gracefield after we catch this lot. Can't if all the servants know what is afoot. The whole town would soon know." This definitely called for another glass of wine.

"They may both be armed. I wish I had Papa's pistol."

"Thing to do, you take my pistol. I'll get a rifle. Too big for a lady to handle." We went to the gun room and selected a gun. Bunny charged it with ammunition, and we smuggled it in the folds of my skirt back to the saloon.

"I hope Fairfield is downstairs by now. It would be easier if we could attack them one by one," I said.

"We'll try Fairfield's room on the way up."

How did a lady summarily invite an invited guest, a lord at that, to quit her house at gunpoint in the middle of the night? I poured another glass of wine. Perhaps it was the surfeit of wine that suggested my next course of action. "Poison!" I exclaimed.

"Eh?"

"I shall poison them."

He considered this a moment. "A bit drastic," he said. "Mean to say, against the law, but a sleeping draft would help. How did you plan to do it? In a bottle of wine?"

"In their feed. I mean the birds, not Snoad and Fairfield. If I poison all the birds, then Snoad cannot send out his false message. By morning we will have met with Depew—" Bunny's shaking head suggested we might never see our mentor again.

"Or whoever is sent to replace him. No doubt that is why no one is watching the house. They have gone to report Depew's death. And whoever they send to replace Depew can handle getting rid of Snoad and Fairfield."

"Do the pigeons feed at night?" he asked.

"No, but first thing in the morning."

"If Caesar arrives tonight, Snoad might send the false message out immediately."

"Then you must take the rifle and stand guard below the loft. If Caesar approaches, shoot him. We'll retrieve the message and give it to Depew, or the man who replaces him."

"By the living jingo, it might just work. Must own—I wasn't looking forward to tackling Snoad. Think I might be able to take Fairfield, but Snoad—gypsies know fighting tricks."

"Before you go outdoors, come up to the loft with me, and just make sure it is empty—of men, I mean. I shall round up all the rat poison I can find and mix it in with the birds' feed."

"I'll go up. You stay here," he said manfully. And I, womanly, had no fault to find with this arrangement.

I went to the pantry where the rat poison is kept, and gathered up a half-empty box and a full one. I met Bunny again in the saloon.

"They're in Snoad's room, both of 'em," he said.

"Could we bar the door?"

"They'd be bound to hear us. I'll nip out and make sure Caesar don't get into the loft while you run up and mix the poison in with the feed."

"You—you wouldn't care to come with me, Bunny?"

"You're safe as a church, my girl. They're into

the brandy. I heard Snoad say he must be back at the loft by two. You have hours to spare."

"I'll come down and tell you when I've finished—just so you know I am safe."

He nodded. "You'll know if you hear a shot that I've winged Caesar."

Bunny was a good shot. He wouldn't miss. Of course, I disliked having to kill Caesar, but between a champion pigeon and the fate of a whole country, there was really no choice. Bunny took the rifle and went out the south door. I took the pistol and my courage and began the long ascent up to the loft. There was no sound from Fairfield's room. I assumed he was still with Snoad. Should I not wait until he had retired? No, this was mere cowardice. With the false courage of three quick glasses of wine, I proceeded on my way.

But I did wish, as I drew open the loft door, that I had insisted Bunny come with me. He could have waited five minutes to begin his lookout for Caesar. In fact, we would have been the first to encounter Caesar if he returned to the loft while we were here. It must have been the wine that made our thinking so fuzzy.

I waited a moment to make sure Snoad was not lurking in the dark. When I had accounted for all the shadows, I moved forward into the loft. A few drowsy birds set up a cooing, but it soon died down. Snoad made sure the feed trays were empty at night, to prevent the pigeons from thinking about food, but the water pans were full. There were three of them: one at either end, and one in the middle. It would make a racket, getting at the feed bags. Snoad kept them in a cupboard behind Caesar's tree. I decided the poison would be as effective in water as in their feed. Pigeons were thirsty birds. I had to set the pistol aside to do the job. I emptied the first partial box into one pan and stirred it up with my finger, as I could find no spoon. Then I tore open the full box and added it to the other two pans, also stirring them.

My heart was thumping like a rabbit's all the time I was there. I was preternaturally alert to any slight sound or motion. A few birds rearranged their feathers. They were either disturbed by my presence, or having pigeon dreams. I waited till they settled down, then began to move on tiptoe to the door. As I reached it, it opened, seemingly of its own volition. My blood turned to wax in my veins. It must be a draft. There hadn't been a sound on the stairs. I waited, heart in my mouth, breath suspended, while the door opened wider.

Then I saw them, Snoad and Fairfield. Fairfield was unarmed, but Snoad carried a gun—Papa's gun. I realized that I had left Bunny's pistol sitting on the floor beside the water pan. In my eagerness to escape, I had forgotten it. We stared at each other for a moment in mutual astonishment. It was Snoad who recovered first.

He leapt in the door, handed Fairfield the gun, clamped an iron hand over my lips, while with the other hand he wrenched my arms behind me. The words he uttered have no place in a polite novel, or in anyone's mouth.

"By God, you were right!" Fairfield said. "You have ears like a fox, Kerwood. I didn't hear anything. What are you doing here, Miss Hume?" He looked with distaste at the rough way Snoad was handling me.

"Take a look around the loft. She's up to something," Snoad ordered.

Fairfield walked up and down. He found the pistol, of course, and the two boxes of rat poison. "My God, she's poisoned the birds!" he exclaimed.

A tide of ugly verbiage even worse than before issued from Snoad's lips. I had never heard such language, even in the stable when the hands didn't know I was nearby. To hear it directed at myself was degrading, and enraging. And to make it worse, I couldn't say a word for the hand that held my mouth closed.

I heard Snoad's heavy breathing behind me. It was more menacing than his oaths. "They don't feed at night," he said. "It must be in the water. Check it."

Fairfield ran to the water pans. "There's something floating here."

"Empty it at once—all three of them."

Fairfield, like a footman, carried the water pans to the mesh grating and sloshed the poisoned water out. I wondered if Bunny was caught in the downpour. If so, he remained silent, but he must be extremely curious. I prayed that he would be curious enough to come and investigate before the half hour was up.

"What are we going to do with her?" Fairfield asked when he had finished his job.

"We'll have to get rid of her," Snoad said flatly.

He spoke of murder as nonchalantly as he might ask for a cup of tea. I made a gagging sound of objection. He pulled my arms harder, and I fell silent. "Take off your cravat," he said to Fairfield. Within a minute, it was tied around my open mouth, tightly lodged between my teeth, preventing any sounds but gargles of outrage.

"There are some ropes in the cupboard behind the tree. Bring me a length" was Snoad's next order.

Fairfield said, "Kerwood, do you really think—"

"Get them."

I tried to wrench my arms free. As that was unsuccessful, I tried to kick him. Between the inefficacy of soft patent slippers and the difficulty of kicking backwards, for Snoad was behind me, that, too, was useless.

Before I knew what was happening, I was trussed up like a goose for the oven, with my arms behind my back, and my feet tied to a pole supporting the pigeon nests. I couldn't even roll or wiggle my way to the stairs and pitch myself down. If I succeeded in moving, I would have the weight of all that lumber on top of me, to say nothing of a hundred angry pigeons.

"What are we going to tell Mrs. Lovatt?" Fairfield demanded. I tried to look innocent, in hopes that Fairfield would take pity and save me.

"We'll make up some tale."

"You are inventive! What can *possibly* account for her disappearance?"

Disappearance was French for death. They were going to kill me. As they would prefer a death that looked accidental, I had the feeling I would soon be flying from the bartizan, to be dashed on the ground below.

"A runaway match," Snoad said indifferently.

"You'd have to go with her in that case."

"I am not the runaway groom I had in mind. I cannot leave, but her disappearance will make an excellent excuse for us to remain here, helping to look for her."

"We'll need a man. Am I it?" Fairfield asked reluctantly.

"Her great friend Depew would be my choice. We know he won't be returning," he said, and laughed.

What had they done to Depew? Good God, if I lived, my reputation would be ruined. I made a growling sound in my throat, while looking daggers at them.

"The idea does not appeal to you, Miss Hume?" Snoad jeered. "You see the truth to the old adage, a person is known by the company she keeps. If you associate with traitors, you cannot expect to escape untarred." His voice rose in anger while he spoke. "Why did you do it?" came out in a howl so loud that Fairfield shushed him.

I tried to spit out my revulsion, but Snoad just laughed. "Let this be a lesson to you, miss. What did he promise you? Fame and glory? Or was it a labor of love? Don't tell me you love that creature. That stretches credulity too far."

On that speech he turned and left, speaking to Fairfield as they strode to the door. "We'll have to get the carriage out of the stable to account for her absence. I'll handle that. You'd best look about for Smythe. We don't want that idiot foiling our plans."

"How long will she have to—"

The door slammed, cutting off Fairfield's question, and Snoad's reply. In my mind, there was no question as to "how long" I would be gone missing. He could not turn me loose after this night's work. He would have to kill me. At the bottom of it all, lurking below the fear, was the insult of Snoad's cavalier response to my being here. I was just an inconvenience. Let this be a lesson to me—as if I had broken some rule of etiquette, and was being sent to my room. He did not even give me the courtesy of outrage, or of grief at losing me.

There wafted at the back of my mind the memory of Snoad's eager lovemaking. "I would marry you if I were king of England, and you a serving wench." He had loved me. What kind of love was it that could calmly speak of "getting rid of her," as though she were a worn-out shoe? It was all an act to con me.

This was no time for useless repining. It would not take long for Snoad to get the carriage out of the stable. My hope rested on Bunny's coming. But what if he did not? What if he thought I had tossed the water over the balcony myself? He would think I had complete freedom of movement up here. I began working on the ropes around my wrists.

The ropes were not so terribly thick. Just jute twine, doubled over six or eight times. Behind me, I felt the rough edge of cut stone that formed the pillar holding up the roof of the widow's walk. It had a sharp edge. I began feverishly working the rope against it. I was scraping my wrists as well, but a few abrasions would not kill me. It seemed an eternity that I sawed the rope against the stone, but when I felt one thickness of twine go, I was heartened, and worked harder, faster. In a few more minutes, I had the ropes off my hands, and untied the cravat that gagged me. I took a few gulps of fresh air and felt better. Getting the ropes off my feet was the hardest part. I could not reach any of the cut stone to sever them, and the knots were small and tight.

I pulled off my slippers, and managed to wiggle

out of the ankle ropes. I immediately darted to the door, only to find it was locked. Trust Snoad to think of that! Fairfield had taken my pistol, so if I remained, I would be at their mercy when they returned. The only hope for escape was the bartizan. With luck, I might see Bunny, and call to him for help. Yet I did not wish to call Fairfield's attention to him. I ran to the edge and peered into the mist. The fog obscured clear vision, but I did not think Bunny was there.

The bartizan was an ornate one, with stone embellishments at intervals that would make good holds for the hands and feet. Snoad had descended by this means, with a rope. The curved bartizan wall went down to within three feet of a little iron balcony outside Papa's bedroom. With luck, and a rope, I might heave myself onto the balcony. I made a quick search for the rope, but in the darkness, I had no luck. I considered the jute twine bindings Snoad had used, but they were not strong enough to carry my whole weight.

Did I have the courage to trust my life to half a dozen stone crockets, which might be perishing and fall off in my hands? The house was ancient. And if I fell, the hard ground was far below. Yet if I stayed, I faced certain death.

Only one solution came to me. I could make a rope long enough to reach the balcony from my gown and petticoat. I would need sure footing, and easy mobility in any case, and should remove those garments. This was not the time for modesty. I stripped down to the barest necessities, even removing my stockings, to give my toes a better grip. I placed the clothing on the railing and leaned out, trying to test the solidity of the first crocket. It was carved from the same piece of stone as the wall, and not attached later as a mere ornament. I pulled at it, and was satisfied that it was firmly fixed. I made the error of looking down, and was struck anew at how far a fall it was if I lost my grip, and my manufactured "rope" failed. Did I really have the iron nerve for this venture?

While I stood, undecided, I heard the key move in the lock. Snoad was back. I had not even begun to tear my gown into strips. I looked around in panic. I must hide myself, hide the clothing.... Hardly knowing what I did, I tossed the clothing over the parapet and ran, looking for someplace to hide. With so little time, the best I could do was to draw back at the far side of the pigeon nests, huddled against the wall. I knew it would take him about two seconds to find me.

Snoad and Fairfield entered together. "He'll be safe there till morning," Fairfield was saying. As Bunny had been Fairfield's job, I assumed he had disabled Bunny in some manner. "Safe till morning" was ambiguous. Did he mean the body would not be discovered till then, or that he was tied up, as I had been?"

The hurrying feet stopped, not two yards from me. If they listened, they would surely hear the booming of my heart. Not a sound was heard. Even the pigeons were still. "She's gone!" Fairfield yelped.

"That's impossible! Take a look around."

My blood curdled. Why hadn't I armed myself? There must be something I could use as a weapon. Snoad hastened to Caesar's tree, and yanked open the cupboard doors behind it. The aroused pigeons associated the sound with food, and began stirring.

Snoad turned and began to rush back to where the jute twine bindings sat on the ground. If he glanced my way, he would see me. We were in a clear line of vision of each other. My white undergarments and pale flesh must stand out against the wooden rows of nests. It was Fairfield who saved me.

"My God!" he exclaimed in disbelief. "We've killed her. She jumped to the ground." He must have seen my gown and petticoat, spread out below. In the fog, they might resemble a body.

Snoad stopped in his tracks. Just such an expression of horror and disbelief must have been frozen on the face of Lot's wife when she was turned into a pillar of salt. He looked like a statue, standing frozen with his mouth open, but no sound issuing from it.

"Come and see!" Fairfield said excitedly. "She's not moving. She'd never survive the jump."

A sobbing "Oh God!" was dragged from the depths of Snoad's being. He lurched forward, toward the parapet of the bartizan. "I've killed her!" he said. It was a howl of anguish, but a very muted howl. "I've killed her. Oh God! What shall I do?"

"We'd best run down. She may still be breathing, but her back is busted for sure."

"Run for a doctor, John."

"Caesar may be winging in any minute."

"Damn Caesar! Go for a doctor, I say."

I heard the clatter of their retreating steps, but I did not move immediately. I stood huddled against the wall, remembering how Snoad had looked when he thought I was dead. I would never forget his expression. He looked desolate, like a man who has killed the one he loves.

Chapter Sixteen

Now was my chance to run. I left the wall and was just hastening toward the door when I became aware of a pigeon fluttering beyond the mesh, waiting to have the trapdoor opened. I went closer, and recognized the hooded crest of Caesar (and, of course, Hector, but it was Caesar who was expected to arrive tonight).

I opened the loft and he came in, cooing in triumph. He settled on his tree, and I went to congratulate him. I spotted the small capsule attached to his leg. He was patient while I tried to remove it. Here another problem faced me. It was held on by a fine wire. I tried to unfasten it, but between darkness and the fumbling of my anxious fingers, I had no luck. Time was short. It would not take the men long to discover their error and come back up.

For lack of a better solution, I took the bird along with the message and ran for the stairs. Caesar disliked this new arrangement. Very likely he was accustomed to some treat after his long flight. I had to hold his beak shut to keep him quiet, and clamped him tightly under my arm to hold his wings steady. A few feathers were dislodged in the process, but I did not take time to cover my tracks.

I was still afraid for my very life. Anxiety will often turn to rage when the anxious one discovers his fear has been unnecessary. Mama boxed my ears when I turned up safe and sound in the attic, after she had convinced herself the gypsies had carried me off. I knew she loved me still, but the release from fear does have that inexplicable effect. What concerned me now was Snoad's ire when he found my empty dress on the ground, and realized I had outwitted him.

I took Caesar to my room and put him in the top drawer of my chest of drawers, where I could retrieve the message later. I closed the drawer, leaving it open a crack lest he should suffocate. My next goal was to reach some safe place where Snoad could not harm me, preferably out of the house altogether. I would run to the constable in Hythe, but first I must find Bunny. In haste I snatched up the first garment that came to hand, which was my blue pelisse. I ran downstairs and left by the road door, the farthest removed from where my gown and petticoat bore testament to my unwitting stunt.

When I stepped out onto the walk, I realized I had come out without shoes or stockings. I stood in the foggy darkness, wondering where my partner was hidden. He had been at the south facade, waiting to shoot Caesar. I gloated that I had got the message. Fate was on the side of the angels, bringing Caesar and his message at a moment when I was alone in the loft. My gloating turned to resignation. There was nothing else for it. I had to go around to the south side. With luck, Fairfield might mention where he had hidden Bunny.

A row of yews had been planted at some far distant time to enhance the south facade of Gracefield. They were old and straggly and unlovely, but they would give some concealment. I edged my way in behind them and crept forward. Sharp stones and fallen needles jabbed at my bare feet. Fairfield and Snoad were still there. Snoad held my gown and petticoat. If he had exploded in wrath upon their discovery, his wrath had simmered down to thoughts of revenge now.

"Where the hell can she be?" he said to Fairfield. "She must be in the house somewhere. I'll turn the place upside down to find her. And when I do!"

"She don't know Depew's been turned in. She might go to the inn after him," Fairfield said.

"Smythe has been there. Cassidy followed him. They know Depew's not around." He had used Cassidy in his vile scheme! He was turning my own servants against me!

"It looks like we must notify Whitehall," Fairfield said.

Whitehall! That suggested they were working for a legitimate English superior. My ears strained to catch Snoad's reply.

"I had a message from Castlereagh this morning. He's spending a few days at home. Cray's Foot is not that far away. You'd best take a jaunt over there, John. Do you know where it is?"

"I've been there a few times."

Viscount Castlereagh was one of the most distinguished gentlemen in the government. He was secretary for foreign affairs, amongst other duties. This paragon was Snoad's superior! It couldn't—it was not possible that I had been duped by Depew. He wore the regalia of the Horse Guards. He knew everything that was going on. He would not have dared to show his nose in the territory of legitimate government agents if he was known to be a traitor. Was that why he had insisted we call him Mr. Martin, and why he was so determined not to be seen? Or was this a new snare devised by Snoad? Did he think I might be listening?

"What will you do?" Fairfield asked.

"Someone has to stay in the loft. Caesar is overdue. We can't let that message go astray."

"Cassidy could do that."

"He's too young and inexperienced. So much depends on it. My own brother Willie is there, in Spain," he said on a weary note. "It is selfish of me, but that bothers me more than the rest." The name struck a familiar note. Someone else had a relative named Willie in Spain. "Are you sure Smythe's bound up right and tight?"

"He won't get loose," Fairfield replied.

"That's what we thought about Heather," Snoad said grimly. "How the hell did she get out?"

"Forget her, Kerwood. She's safe somewhere. I blame it on Depew. He has an insinuating way with the ladies. She doesn't know what is going on. Has no idea she was aiding Boney. Depew duped her. You should have told her the truth from the beginning." *I* was helping Boney? This was heinous!

"You'd better go on, John," Snoad said. "Just check that Smythe's still breathing, will you? We don't want to kill the idiot."

I was still trying to think through the intricacies of my position, and wondering if I should come out of the yews. If I came forward now, they might immediately gag me again.

They parted. I followed Fairfield, to learn where he had sequestered Bunny. He took a quick jaunt down to a shed near the water that was last used in the days when the Humes were boatsmen. It held sails and masts and rigging equipment. He opened the door with a squawk, went in, and immediately came out again. As soon as he was gone, I rushed in, calling Bunny's name.

A shaft of light from an unglazed window showed me a hump on the floor which turned out to be Bunny, trussed up and gagged as I had been. They had removed his own cravat to gag him, and used ropes left over from days of yore. First I removed the gag, and he made some strangled sounds as he gasped for a good lungful of air.

"They got me!" he gasped. "Are you all right?"

"I'm all right now." I began working at the bindings around his wrists.

"I wondered when that water came cascading over the balcony. What was you doing?"

"Fairfield did it. I had put the rat poison in the water troughs. They caught me."

Eventually I freed his wrists. He rubbed them back into circulation and freed his own ankles. He tried to stand up, but immediately fell down again. "Feet feel pierced by a thousand needles," he said, and wiggled them around a moment.

While he worked himself back into shape, I outlined my adventures.

"They gave me a stunning blow from behind," he explained. "Didn't hear a sound as he crept up on me. A tree branch, I believe he used. Knocked me out cold. When I woke up, I was here. Wherever here is. Where the deuce are we?"

"In the suds," I said. "The horridest thing, Bunny. It is Depew who is the French spy, and we have been helping him."

"He had the buttons, and the yaller lining."

"He probably stole them from someone he murdered. We must go somewhere safe where we can talk. Snoad might check here."

"If they've got us pegged for traitors, England ain't safe. We'll have to go abroad."

"We have to get out of this shed for a start," I said, and we went out into the night air. The shingle was uncomfortable underfoot, cold and hard. I had to pick my way along.

As we rounded the corner of the boat shed, we noticed that the windows of Gracefield were all ablaze with lights. The various comings and goings had woken everyone up. By now Snoad might be telling Auntie that I had run away with Depew. My heart sank to consider what her worries must be. This was worse than being carried off by gypsies.

Worst of all was that Snoad despised me. I didn't know who or what he was, but I knew, I had always sensed really, that he was a gentleman. Fairfield deferred to him. He called him Kerwood, and Snoad called him John, like friends. The Duchess of Prescott had befriended him. The duchess! That was who had a son called Willie in the Peninsula! And Snoad had a brother of the same name. All those letters from Branksome Hall—he was the duchess's son.

And we had stuck him up under the eaves in a couple of rooms filled with cast-off furnishings. We had called him Snoad, and condescended to him. What a wretched stunt to pull on a lady! Auntie did not know it. Of that I was dead certain, but Papa had known. The government had set the whole thing up, with Snoad helping Papa under an alias. I did not know why an alias was necessary, except that a nobleman staying at Gracefield for the duration of the war would, of course, cause a great stir, and they wished for secrecy. It was well known, too, that the duchess was an expert pigeon breeder. That could account for it. Snoad (soon I would know his real name) must be a great expert in this carrier pigeon business. Papa had raced them, but Snoad was the expert.

"Can you walk, or do you want my boots?" Bunny asked.

I could not think such huge, heavy things would be better than my bare feet, and declined the offer. We strolled at random away from the house, toward Hythe, while I discussed the details of the past days with Bunny. The odd thing is that he accepted the incredible story without blinking.

"We always thought Depew was a pretty inferior sort of a spy," he said. "Daresay he was the one broke into your papa's study and stole his gun."

"Snoad had Papa's gun, but Depew may have broken into the house."

"We know he left Brighton before we did. He never got the message you sent him."

"He was looking for the code book, I expect. That was what he wanted from us all along, and feeding us praise to keep us in line. I imagine he made up that story about Snoad searching the house with a light, to keep us looking. It was the message from Caesar he hoped to get his hands on. And we would have handed it over to him. He never had any men in our park. All lies."

"Regular Johnnie Raws. Caesar didn't show up anyhow. Not while I was waiting for him."

"Oh lord, *Caesar!*"

"He'll turn up yet."

"He has turned up. He's in my dresser drawer."

"Eh? I must be going deaf. I thought you said—"

"I did! We must go back, Bunny. I have to give Snoad that message."

"We could sneak in and have a servant give it to him. Leave a note in your room addressed to Snoad. Put your shoes on while you're there. And a dress," he added. "Thing for us to do, I believe, light out for America. Won't be easy, with this war on. Better than hanging. Catch a fishing trawler to get out of the country, transfer somewhere in midocean."

"We haven't done anything wrong. We were duped!"

"Who'll believe that? We'll look a dashed pair of fools."

"That is better than looking like traitors. I'm going back."

"I'll drop you a line from America."

"You must come with me and corroborate my story. Flight will be taken as evidence of real guilt. And we have Caesar," I added. "When we turn the message over, they will know our hearts are in the right place. We could have taken it and run— somewhere," I said, at a loss as to what we might have done with it.

"Could use the note for barter, I daresay. Our lives for the letter. Have to secure the letter somewhere first. Might torture us to make us talk. This spying game is a little dirtier than I thought. Don't believe I'll offer my services after all. Not that they'd want me now."

"Are you coming or not?" I demanded. His chatter was depressing me greatly. "I must give that message to Snoad. And Auntie will be worried sick that I've made a runaway match."

Bunny stood, undecided. "Daresay I must go with you. Not the thing, abandoning a lady in distress. As you said, we're only dupes, not traitors."

On this speech we turned and retraced our steps to Gracefield. Despite my encouragement, my heart was as unwilling as Bunny's. I was humiliated to present myself in such a ridiculous guise to Snoad. Not only a dupe, but a dupe with a dirty face, without a gown, and in her bare feet.

Chapter Seventeen

We went to the door that led to the kitchen. It was locked, but lights were on within. I tapped, and Mrs. Gibbons came. She had changed from nightgown to dress and apron, but had forgotten to remove her nightcap. It was of white flannel, tied beneath her chin like a baby's bonnet.

"Merciful heavens, Miss Hume! You're back!" she said, and pulled me inside. Bunny trailed in behind me. "I knew it would be you," she said, examining him with relief before returning her sharp eyes in my direction. "Mr. Depew indeed! Whoever heard of a Mr. Depew? As if you would marry a stranger." She gave Bunny a tentative smile. "But Mr. Smythe is your first cousin, my dear. You should have got a dispensation from the bishop. First cousins are forbidden kindred for marriage."

In the light of the kitchen, she discerned my bare feet, and noticed that no gown showed at the front of my pelisse. "Good gracious! You could have waited till you found a bed at least! Look at you. You must have been—"

"Don't be absurd, Mrs. Gibbons," I declared, in my most haughty tone. "I did not run away with Mr. Smythe. I was abducted, and he rescued me." I had to give some excuse for my appearance.

Her shock did not subside, but it assumed an air of satisfaction. Abduction, it seemed, was preferable to a runaway marriage. "I'll call your auntie. She's in hysterics, poor soul. That wretched Snoad has been filling her ears with tales of your running off with Depew. She was cheered to learn Lord Fairfield had gone after you."

So that was what he had told her. How did he mean to account for it when Castlereagh arrived and led me away in chains? Was he trying to protect me by claiming the lesser evil? Did some spark of love still remain, or was it only chivalry?

"Was it Depew who kidnapped you?" Mrs. Gibbons asked.

Caught off guard, I said, "Yes," then quickly spoke on to divert further questions. "Let me slip up the back stairs and get dressed, before I see Auntie. And would you have some hot water sent up, please? I'm filthy."

Mrs. Gibbons nodded her agreement. She was sufficiently recovered to offer Bunny a cup of tea.

"Don't mind if I do," I heard him say. "That gag has made my throat sore." It was a nasty stunt to leave Bunny to fabricate the tale of my kidnapping. Imagination was never his long suit.

I scampered up the servants' stairs, into the hallway. The carpet was kind to my bruised feet. It felt like walking on a cloud, after the roughness of stones and earth. I noticed that my wrists were chafed and bleeding where the stone had scraped them. They would sting like the devil when I washed up. I hurried along the empty hallway to my room and threw open the door, without a thought in my mind but washing and dressing. One step at a time.

Imagine my astonishment to find Mr. Snoad there, holding my dressing gown, and staring at it as if it might speak. His eyes, wide with disbelief, flew to mine. He didn't speak for a moment, nor could I think of how to begin my explanations. We just stared at each other, while the clock ticked in the yawning silence. I felt those coffee-dark eyes were plumbing the very depths of my soul. I would never forget their bleak, accusing gaze.

Then he dropped my dressing gown on the floor and closed the door. "So you're back," he said in a harsh voice.

Tears stung my eyes. "I didn't know," I said. My hands went out to him in an involuntary gesture. In the same involuntary way, he reached for them. Before we touched, he recovered himself and withdrew a step from me, as one withdraws from a snake or venomous creature.

I watched in misery as his lips thinned to a cruel line, and his spine stiffened to intransigence. "I'm not easily conned a second time, Miss Hume. Not even by you. *You knew*. You knew everything. Why else did you search my room? Why else did you try to poison the birds? How did he convince you?"

"You mean Depew?"

"Of course I mean Depew!" he growled. His next words came out in an angry rush. "I have been racking my brain for some slight shred of excuse for what you have done. While I thought you were dead, I could forgive you. Blame it on your youth, your sorrow and anger at your father's death. I called it a childish, ill-conceived attempt at revenge for that accident. But you are no child, Miss Hume. And your father is not the only man who has given his life for his country. The other grieving wives and daughters did not turn traitor. Just tell me one thing. Was it for love or money that you traded your soul to Satan?"

"Enough!" I shouted. My spine, too, was stiff. I, too, had my anger to vent, and now it was my turn. Snoad's eyes widened in surprise at my new attitude. "If my attempts to help were childish and ill conceived, they were at least not ignoble. I *did* agree to help Depew, because I thought he was helping England. He wore the prince's buttons. He said, and Mr. Smythe corroborated, that Depew was with the Horse Guards."

Snoad listened, but with an air of suspicion that he did not even try to conceal. "So he was—six months ago, when he came under suspicion. He was a junior clerk, who was caught rifling files he had no right to see. Nothing was proven, but he was turned out. Since then, he's been watched. We put abroad the idea that Fairfield was in financial trouble. Depew approached Fairfield as a possible ally. Fairfield was assigned the job of keeping an eye on him."

"Why was everything kept a secret from me? I had a right to know. You have been using my house."

"With Mr. Hume's permission."

"What was I to think, when my father's simple trip to a meeting in London resulted in his assassination in Brighton?"

"Secrecy was necessary. We did not wish to draw attention to what was going on at Gracefield. There are many spies here on the coast. When you vowed revenge for your father's death, we felt you were too—volatile—to trust with the truth. Hotheads have no place in this service."

"You did not trust me because I was a woman," I said bluntly, for I felt that was the real reason. "You could trust a simpleton like Fairfield, but you could not trust me."

His suspicion assumed an air of apology. "Your actions from the moment you returned from Brighton hardly encouraged trust. Your first suggestion was to get rid of the loft. Why the rush, if you didn't know what it was being used for? Then your friend Depew broke into the house."

"It would not have been necessary for him to *break* in if he were my friend," I pointed out.

"You had not returned yet. I assumed he was in a hurry to have a look at your father's papers. And if you wished to keep your association with him a secret from me, as you obviously did, then you could hardly introduce him into the house as a friend."

"He did not want you or anyone to know he was here. He called himself Mr. Martin."

"I observed that all your meetings were carried on with some attempt at secrecy. I thought no worse of you than that you were Depew's dupe, playing at being a spy. Of course, Depew was followed and watched, and his movements reported to Fairfield. Until you arranged that ambush at Atherton, I was willing to blink at your little game. When you connived at my assassination—" His tirade came to a halt, and he stared angrily. "How *could* you, knowing how I felt about you?"

I felt as bad as if I were indeed guilty of these awful crimes. "I had no idea he meant to shoot you. He said you would be meeting your colleagues. He wanted to round up the whole crew."

Snoad rubbed his hand over his forehead and drew a deep sigh. "If this is true—"

"Of course it's true!" I shouted.

That was the moment his doubts left him. I could see it mirrored on his face as the truth penetrated. Suspicion flickered as some few details occurred to him, but apparently he found reassurance. The shadow of a smile moved his lips. And at that pregnant moment the servants came to the door with a basin of hot water.

It would scandalize them to find me half-dressed, with a man in my room. Snoad looked at me. I don't think he had even realized till then that I wore no gown under my pelisse. I pointed to the clothespress, and without a word spoken, Snoad fled into it as I went to open the door.

Mrs. Gibbons had sent up a large boiler of water, which necessitated a footman to carry it. Her nice sense of delicacy required Mary, a female servant, to accompany him on this intimate errand. They arranged the bath while I held my pelisse tightly around me, and tried, quite unsuccessfully, not to draw attention to my bare feet.

"Are you all right, Miss Hume?" Mary asked before leaving. I thought she showed great restraint to limit herself to this mild question.

"I'm fine. Thank you."

They left, and Snoad came out of the clothespress. Such was his sangfroid that he was not even blushing. He was slightly ill at ease, or uncertain how to deal with the new situation, but mostly he was curious about my appearance. His eyes moved questioningly from my tousled head, down my wrinkled pelisse, to my dirty feet. I was acutely aware of what an unappetizing picture I presented, and spoke sharply.

"Do you believe me?" I asked, fixing him with a steely eye.

"It could have happened that way," he admitted. When his eyes veered off to the left, I thought he was merely being kind by not staring at me.

"It did happen that way. How could you think I would connive at murder? Or betray my country? My family have lived here, in this very house, for over two hundred years. I love every tree and bush, every pebble on the beach. I was proud of my father's death. I was willing to risk my own life to complete his work, and this is the thanks I get. I was only poisoning the pigeons so you could not send false messages to Bonaparte. And the only reason I searched your room was because Depew told me to try to find the code book you were using."

"Of course. If Depew convinced you he was working for England, it must follow that I was on the other side. You accuse me of misjudging you, but you are guilty of the same error." Again, he peered over my shoulder. A frown drew his brows together.

"What are you looking at?" I followed his gaze, and saw he was staring at my dresser. Through the crack left for Caesar to breathe, a pair of eyes and a beak protruded from the top drawer. Caesar recognized Snoad, and became quite excited.

"Is that—is that a *pigeon* in your dresser?" he asked.

"Oh! Caesar! I hope he is not asphyxiated."

"Caesar!" he exclaimed. "When did he get in?"

He flew to the dresser and retrieved the bird, who had remained amazingly calm throughout the entire ordeal. Perhaps he had been sleeping after his long flight. His hood feathers were slightly disarranged from his incarceration, but they righted themselves once he was free. Snoad reached in his trousers pocket and drew out a handful of grain. He placed it and the bird on the corner of the dresser and let Caesar peck at it while he removed the message. It came off easily, as he knew the trick of unfastening it.

"When did he get in?" Snoad repeated. He slid the capsule containing the message into his pocket.

"He came while you and Fairfield left me tied up in the loft."

Snoad looked up at me through his lashes. An angry smile quirked at his lips. "That was a vile stunt, Heather, letting me think I had killed you."

"Much you would care! Will you please take your bird out of here? I want to have my bath."

He picked Caesar up and held him under one arm, as if he were a book, or a ball. "I'm leaving. I have to send a reply to this message. And afterwards—what shall we tell Mrs. Lovatt?"

"The truth. Now go."

He seemed much inclined to stay. I shooed him out and closed the door. I had convinced Snoad. Now it was up to him to convince Lord Castlereagh that I was not fodder for the gallows. Before I saw anyone else, I must remove the soil of this night's misadventures.

The reflection in the mirror showed me a woman who looked as if she had been crawling through mud. My face and pelisse were streaked with grime, and my hair all tumbled loose. One had to wonder why this wreck of humanity was smiling.

I removed my clothes and slid into the tub. The warm water closed over me, but my feet and wrists stung where the skin was broken. Soap was a torment to them. I made a hasty bath, and as I toweled myself dry, I chose my gown. I had not the least idea what Snoad had done with the black gown I had been wearing. What hung in my closet were colored gowns, and as I must breach the proprieties, I chose the most attractive of them. A pale rose with rutched skirt and pale green ribbons always elicited praise.

A duke's son had to be impressed by my toilette when I went belowstairs. Auntie would forgive everything when she learned Snoad's true identity. And still I did not know his real name, but I was glad it was not Snoad. I did not want to go through life as Mrs. Snoad. Perhaps I would be Lady Kerwood, depending on Snoad's position in the hierarchy of the Duke of Prescott's sons.

The sun rose while I had my bath. I had not had my head on a pillow all night, but I was not at all sleepy.

Chapter Eighteen

I was just putting the finishing touches on my coiffure when Auntie burst into my room. "Heather! Is it true?" she demanded. "Snoad is the Duke of Prescott's son?"

"Oh, he told you. Yes, it is true."

That was the feature of the whole affair that rode uppermost in her mind. Never mind that I had been embroiled in a wretched affair with a traitor, and nearly lost my life. Never mind that Gracefield was playing an integral part in winning the war. We had been entertaining an eligible peer unawares, and an angel could not have been more welcome.

"I knew from the way he handled the cards that he was no commoner. Did I not say that he was very gentlemanly in his behavior? And to think, we have stuck him up in the attic these two years! I have told Mrs. Gibbons to have the Gold Suite turned out."

"Fairfield is in the Gold Suite. We cannot chuck him out."

"Bother! Then it must be the Green Room, but as soon as Fairfield leaves, we shall remove Snoad—Lord Maitland—into the Gold Suite. The eldest son, a marquess," she added. "He will inherit the dukedom and half a dozen estates. I could not like to quiz him, but surely the Prescotts are top of the trees."

I was as thrilled as Aunt Lovatt, but not quite so voluble. A maiden dare not crow until she had had an offer. "I would marry you if I were the king of England," he had said. Surely that was a sort of offer?

"My dear!" she exclaimed as she examined me for fitness to entertain a marquess. "You cannot wear a pink dress. We are in mourning, and Lord Castlereagh is coming. Fairfield has gone to fetch him. Something to do with a message to be sent to Spain. So very exciting. Do you think a green goose for dinner, or would braised hens be better for the fowl dish? No, Cook's green goose is unexceptionable."

"My black gown is—torn," I said. I did not know how much Snoad—I would go on thinking of him as Snoad—had told her, but I doubted she was privy to the entire affair.

"I'll lend you my black cashmere shawl. I daresay Lord Castlereagh will not even meet you. I have had Smythe's truckle bed taken out of your father's study. The gentlemen can have their meeting there. Lord Maitland assures me Lord Castlereagh will not be staying to dinner." —Auntie had little trouble switching to the preferred name.— "Perhaps luncheon, he said. I must rush down to Mrs. Gibbons. Was there ever such a day! And to think I had despaired of getting you bounced off satisfactorily, when Fairfield turned out to be such a disappointment." Fairfield was now permitted to be the simpleton he was.

She turned and dashed to the door, then turned back. "It all has to do with the pigeons, you see," she informed me. "Something about war messages sent abroad, but it is a great secret. Not a word to anyone, even the servants. Imagine, those stupid birds being such a blessing in disguise." An echo of delighted laughter hung on the air after she left.

I soon followed her downstairs. I felt self-conscious, and shy of meeting Snoad. I wondered how he would behave. I need not have worried. He wasn't there. Bunny was. Mrs. Gibbons had endeavored to make him presentable. He told me that Snoad had ridden out to meet Lord Castlereagh.

"I lent him my mount," he explained. "Mean to say, since our lives depend on him. I thought it best to butter him up any way I could. Seemed very civil, considering."

"I believe I have convinced him of the truth, Bunny."

"He believes *you*. *You're* a woman. He half suspects I was in league with Depew. Told him about the prince's buttons. Said Depew had to turn 'em in. Either stole someone else's, or had a set forged. I noticed he didn't dare wear 'em but the once, to fool us. What was a man to think? Prince's own buttons."

"Where is Depew?"

"Arrested yesterday in Atherton. Followed Snoad and Fairfield. Explains why he didn't want my escort. Hid behind a tree and took a couple of shots at 'em. Fairfield winged him. They caught him, and turned him in. He fed Snoad a load of rubbish that we was in on the whole thing. Spiteful wretch! Been thinking—you remember how excited Depew was at Brighton when he heard your father's body came from London? He must have figured the Horse Guards did it. Was worried they'd learn something."

"Yes, and we know now why he did not want us listening at doors, too—in case we learned the truth."

"Can't count on Depew to back us up. There's always America. I ought to go home and pack, just in case."

"I'm sure it will be all right."

"I'm not. Not by a jugful. Soon as Snoad brings back my mount, I'll scramble off home. You'll let me know how it turns out? A note in the blasted pine . . ." he added, with a wan smile at our folly. "It was a nice adventure, wasn't it, Heather?"

"A lovely adventure."

We discussed it a little longer, until we heard the sound of a carriage heralding Lord Castlereagh's arrival. Bunny went and hid in the cellar, in case he might be arrested. I felt Kerwood had gone to meet Castlereagh to save us that gentleman's ill humor when the truth was revealed. I could only assume he had done his job uncommonly well.

Lord Castlereagh was charm personified. Instead of menaces and manacles, he came in with smiles and compliments. The likenesses I had seen of him did not begin to do the man justice. He had such an air of dignity, and such well-tailored jackets, that he quite bowled Auntie over. And such names as dropped from his lips! "The Prince Regent was saying t'other night," and "As Liverpool mentioned to me in cabinet" were impressive, but it was his nonchalant mention of Princess Caroline and Lady Jersey that put us ladies on the edge of our seats. From his conversation, I cannot think he knew a single commoner. It was all royalty and nobility that he spoke of.

Just before he retired to Papa's study with Kerwood and Fairfield, he grasped my hand and shook it. "Young Maitland tells me it was you who secured the message from Caesar, Miss Hume. Well done! You have performed an invaluable service for your country."

"Thank you, milord," I said in a breathless voice. My eyes flew to Kerwood, standing behind Lord Castlereagh. He smiled and shrugged, as if to say, "All in a day's work."

"Mr. Smythe was also helpful," Kerwood said. "Where is Mr. Smythe, Heather?"

"He—had to step out. He will be back presently."

I sent off to the cellar to tell him the coast was clear. He was very much relieved to hear the news. "Any chance of that baronetcy?" he asked, flying from despair to foolish optimism.

"For that, you will have to volunteer your continuing services."

"Believe I'll pass. A nice little adventure, but I wouldn't care for a steady diet of being tied up and beaten."

Lord Castlereagh honored us by remaining for luncheon, and praising everything on the table to the skies. Yet I was not disappointed when he said he was afraid he would have to eat and run. Urgent matters awaited him at Whitehall. He got me aside again and said, "I do not like to impose on your good nature, Miss Hume, but would it be possible to continue using Gracefield as a relay point until Maitland can arrange another spot?"

It took me a moment to realize that Maitland was Snoad. And he was planning to leave! "You are welcome to use it as long as necessary, milord," I assured him. "Indeed I cannot imagine why you would want to change relay points, when everything is in operation here."

"I own that was what I hoped you would say," he replied, with a triumphant look in Kerwood's direction. "Your father, I feel, would want it so. A brave man. His death was a tragedy that was strongly felt at Whitehall. He would be proud of you."

Then he bowed, and went to say a few parting words to Mrs. Lovatt and Bunny. Fairfield was to follow him to London. Kerwood accompanied them out to their carriages. When he returned, he said he had business to attend to in the loft. His eyes moved to mine. I read, or imagined, that he wished me to accompany him.

"I'll be toddling along," Bunny said. "Mama will want to hear all about Lord Castlereagh. Is it all right to mention he was here? I know the rest of it is a great secret."

Kerwood accompanied him to the door, talking intently as they went. I assumed he was warning Bunny that he could not betray a word of what he had witnessed. Whether the servants would be similarly mute was another matter. There had been no bones about calling Lord Castlereagh by an assumed name, or pretending he was just a passing friend or relative.

"Would you care to join me for a few moments in the loft, Heather?" Kerwood asked when he returned.

No frown creased my chaperone's brow. Her face was wreathed in encouraging smiles.

"Yes indeed," I said at once. "I shall take more interest in Papa's work in future. Perhaps I can lend you a hand with the pigeons from time to time."

Kerwood offered his arm, and we moved to the staircase. While we were still within Auntie's earshot, he spoke most discreetly. "That would be very kind of you. There are times when I would welcome a little break." As we mounted higher, the words took a more indecorous turn. "Or even a little company. It is lonesome up there, alone in the clouds. I cannot think of anyone whose company I would enjoy more."

"We shall assign you whatever help you require. Another footman could easily be spared."

"A footman is not what I meant, wretch," he said, pinching my arm.

We reached the loft, and he held the door for me. "Alone at last!" he said. As soon as the door was closed, he pulled me into his arms. "I thought Castlereagh would hang on forever."

His lips found mine and we embraced, up in the clouds, with the pigeons cooing in approval. I had feared that the embrace would have lost some of its charm, now that Snoad was Maitland, and perfectly respectable. That thrill of the forbidden would be gone, is what I mean. That particular aura was indeed missing, but the relief of knowing it was my future husband who assaulted my lips more than compensated for it. Thrills and danger were still there in plentiful supply.

"Let us go out on the bartizan," I said. It was a more romantic spot.

The ocean gleamed like tarnished silver in the distance, and the breeze carried the tang of the sea. We took one look at the view, then came together again. As naturally as breathing, his arms enfolded me, and I put my arms around him. It seemed both natural and miraculous all at once, that I should be there with Snoad.

"What's your name?" I asked, and laughed at the absurdity of not knowing.

"Kerwood. I knew Fairfield would blurt it out, so decided to call myself Kerwood, as I had never been called by any Christian name here. Fairfield had been at Branksome Hall a few times. He knew I was working here, but was unaware of the alias I had assumed. I didn't want him to reveal the truth."

"So that is why you rushed in to establish that you were posing as a servant from Branksome Hall. I thought it uncommonly encroaching of you. Is Kerwood Snoad your name?"

"Milverton is my family name."

"Kerwood Milverton. Why did you choose a horrid name like Snoad?"

He looked at the scratches on my wrists, and shook his head. Then he lifted my hands and kissed the scratches. "You ought to put something on them," he said, before answering my question. "Why was I called Snoad? It seemed to suit the person I had to become. Once I met you, I regretted I had chosen such a lowly disguise. I might have been a gentleman scholar instead. It was really up to me. I wanted to be able to correspond with Mama without much difficulty, so I pretended I had worked for her, and that made me a servant."

"Why not come as yourself?"

"The powers that be feared my presence might elicit curiosity, and gossip. It is well known in some places that my mother and I breed famous homing pigeons. That is why Branksome Hall was considered ineligible as a relay point. A sharp marksman could pick the pigeons out of the sky as they neared home. Your father bred racers, easily converted to homing pigeons without anyone being the wiser. We made a point to continue racing some birds. If Lord Maitland had suddenly moved in, however, it would not have been long before the real reason for my being here seeped out."

"I fear there will be gossip over Lord Castlereagh's visit," I said. It was hard to carry on a sensible conversation with Kerwood nipping at my ears and nuzzling my throat, and holding me tightly against him.

"It is not a secret. In fact, I think we ought to have it put in the local journal."

I thought he was joking, and slapped his wrist. "Surely that is going a little far!"

He grabbed my hand and squeezed it. "Not at all. He came to meet Lord Maitland's fiancée. Ah, did I remember to propose, Miss Hume? I recall your sad words that you must marry a gentleman. Was that the only impediment to our match?"

His cocky assurance required a setdown. "Certainly not. I have upped my demands to a title. Your potential dukedom will do, I daresay."

"Sorry I couldn't be a prince. I'll try to be charming at least. A duke charming." He bowed playfully.

"But no one knows you are Lord Maitland."

"They can know it now. My being engaged to

you—soon married, I hope—gives me an unexceptionable reason to be here. All the world loves a lover, you must know. They will not suspect skulduggery from one."

"How did I meet you?"

"Why, it was that race your father went to in Bath a year ago. I was struck dumb at your beauty. Couldn't get you out of my mind. In fact, I have been composing verses to your charms ever since, as you, I think, are well aware?"

"Love verses? I thought they were spy messages."

"Really!" he said, offended. "I'll show them to you. They're quite marvelous."

"They were horrid. And I do not have gray eyes. They are green."

"Memory played me false. I didn't get much chance to gauge your *beaux yeux*." He examined them then. "They do have a tint of gray—a reflection from the sky, I think."

"I thought it was some sort of code. I hardly noticed they rhymed. And furthermore, I didn't go to Bath with Papa for that race."

"Nor did I. No one will remember. And I trust no one outside of this house will recognize me as Snoad, once I am properly outfitted. I haven't met many people. In any case, all this won't be for long. Wellington is chasing the French over the Alps. Within the year, it will be all over. Lord Maitland, of course, cannot spend all his time at the loft. You will want to parade your trophy amongst your friends. In a small way, of course, considering we are in mourning."

I was gratified that he said "we." I think he really was fond of Papa.

"I'll have Mama send some trained men to oversee the routine work," he added. "I can handle the sending of the messages."

"Where do you hide the code book, Kerwood?"

"In here," he said, and drew a tiny little book from his inner pocket. It was two inches by three, as Depew had said, but thin enough to lie flat without causing a bulge. "Depew must have got wind that an important message was on the way. Anyone who studies the journals knows a crisis is approaching. He meant to kill me and Fairfield, and get into the loft to intercept it. He knew from his days at the Horse Guards that the messages were coded. They would have been no good to him without this."

"I expect that is what he was looking for when he broke into my father's office."

"I would think so. I took the gun before Depew came. I went after it the night I met you there. After your father's murder, I felt it was well to be armed. I returned later and got it. I wanted to tell you the truth that night."

"Why didn't you?"

"My orders were to tell no one. Later, I learned that you had met Depew in Brighton. He has coerced or duped patriotic people to help him before. You were angry at your father's death. If you felt the men using him had let him down—well, people have acted from revenge before now. But really, until the ambush, I felt you were an innocent dupe. That felt like a betrayal, though one really ought to put the good of the country above personal feelings."

I wondered if I would have sacrificed Kerwood for the good of the country. I was glad I did not have

213

to make the choice. "How did my father come to die, Kerwood? Who killed him?"

"Fairfield told me, after you had fed me that foolish story about his being at the fish market, that your father returned to change for dinner and caught Depew searching his room. For a message, or the code book, or even something he could use as blackmail. Depew had a gun. Your father turned to bolt out the door for help. Depew lost his head and shot him. He then dashed a water jug to the floor to explain the noise if a servant came to check. A passing servant did stop, I believe. She mistook Depew for the legal occupant of the room, and thought little of it. We had a man in the hotel. He investigated the noise and soon learned of the death. He missed Depew, but he managed to get hold of the pigeon cages from the stable. They wanted to salvage those valuable trained homing pigeons."

"And it was your man who said my father had died of a heart attack?"

"Yes, to conceal that he was involved in spying. Everything about the business is kept dark. Mrs. Mobley came to the hotel shortly after, asking for him. She was told he had had some sort of stroke, and died. Then, of course, it was impossible to have a local doctor, in case she learned the truth. So his body was taken to London. Unfortunately, his case got left behind in the rush."

"Why did you want his boots? Did you think there was a message in them?"

"No, I didn't want them, actually. Williams offered them to me. I could find no excuse to refuse such a generous gift without inciting curiosity, so I accepted them. Cassidy tells me they will just fit his papa."

"Was my father delivering a message when he was killed?"

"Not that time. He was merely delivering our birds, to be conveyed to the next relay point, on the south tip of France, and receiving birds for us to send out messages. Sometimes he did deliver or receive messages from London to bring me. We liked to vary the means and the messenger. There was some trouble with the relay point in London—they suspected a leak, and weren't sure at the time who it was. But that was straightened out, and we were flying the messages on to London again. We never dreamed your father was in mortal danger, or we would not have let him go alone. He wanted to do it. He was . . . seeing Mrs. Mobley in Brighton, and so it was convenient."

"That woman has been the bane of our lives. She nearly destroyed Papa's marriage when Mama found out he was seeing her. I cannot imagine why he would want to see her again."

"A man gets lonesome. Shall I tell you about the nights I have spent up here, thinking about you? And when at last you began calling, I had to mistrust you."

"That did not seem to deter you much," I reminded him.

"You are very much mistaken. I felt I could finally tell you who I was, and how I felt—only to learn you had become Depew's unwitting ally."

"You should have told me. Nobody tells me anything. One would think I were a child."

"I cannot speak for the others, but I no longer think anything of the sort. I would never do—this to a child," he said, and kissed me in a very mature fashion.

There is definitely some magic in the loft. The ocean breeze floats over you. The soft waves lap on the shore below, hinting at eternity, while all around the doves coo like love birds. And, of course, it will always be associated in my mind with Kerwood, and his own special brand of danger.